STURGIS & BEYOND
WITH JOE & HIS HARLEY, PORKCHOP

ISBN 978-0-615-48303-0

Second Edition September 10th 2012

STURGIS & BEYOND WITH JOE & HIS HARLEY, PORKCHOP

AN ADVENTURE

BY

JOE MATUS

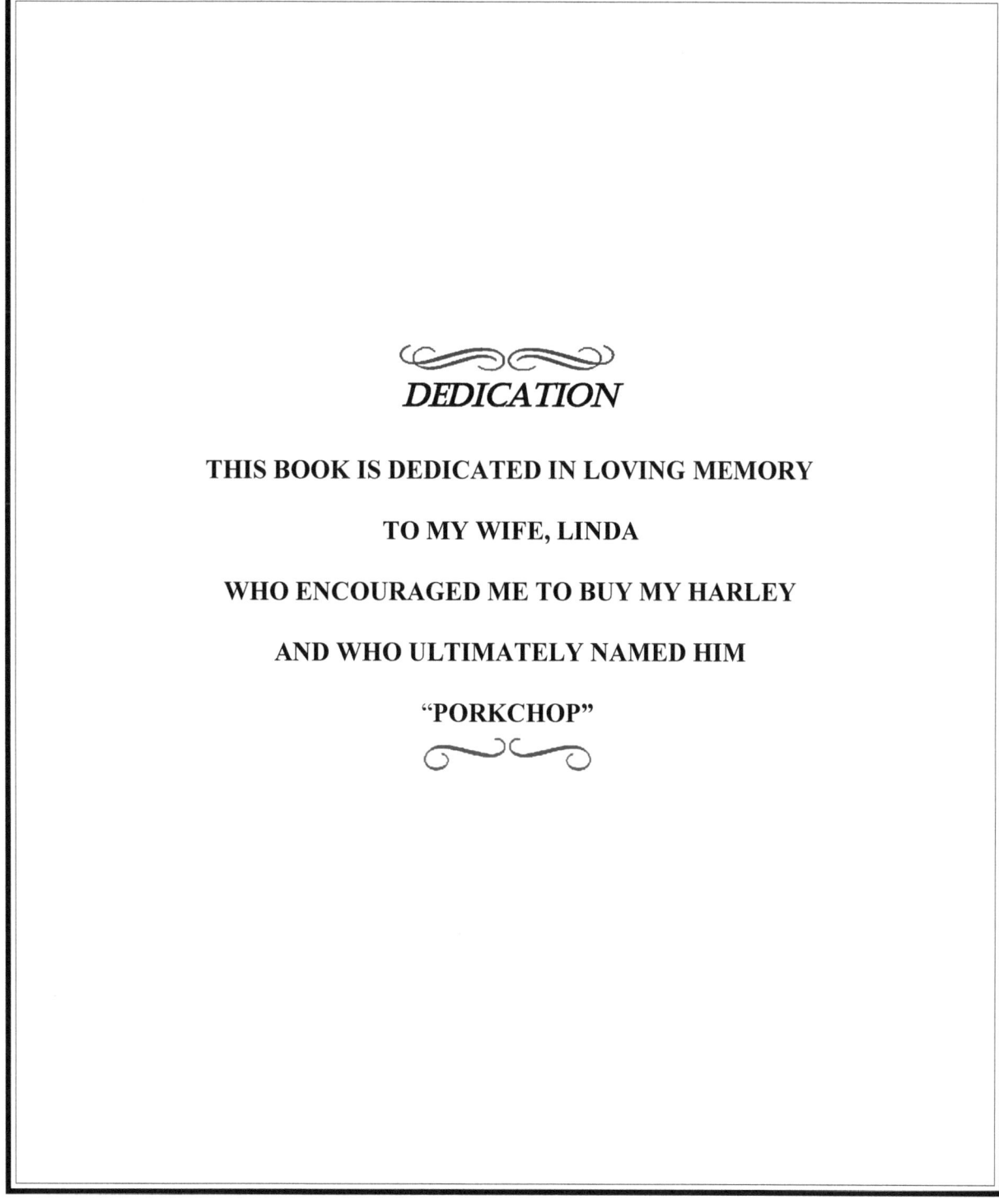

DEDICATION

THIS BOOK IS DEDICATED IN LOVING MEMORY

TO MY WIFE, LINDA

WHO ENCOURAGED ME TO BUY MY HARLEY

AND WHO ULTIMATELY NAMED HIM

"PORKCHOP"

PROLOGUE

MY MOTTO IS:

We only have one life to live, but if you do it right, ONE IS ALL YOU NEED.

∞

The genesis of this book was the desire to share with my grandchildren the great joy of adventure. I wanted to inspire them with the idea that risk, courage and resourcefulness pay great dividends and that if their Grandpa could take this ride all by himself and have a blast doing it, then they too could do anything. I wanted to put more context into the photos than, 'here I am at Mt. Rushmore and here I am standing by this tree' etc. So I created fictional characters to go along with the photos that I emailed every evening at the end of my ride. I crafted this story in such a way as to inform and entertain them, plus anyone else who wishes to seek adventure.

I wanted them to develop an interest about the trip, and on that note, I'll also be providing them with highlighted maps of the trip with all the places I stopped for gas and every restaurant I had stopped for a meal, etc. My hopes are, that in the distant future my great, great, grandkids will look at this and perhaps say, "Man, our great, great, Grandpa had a lot of guts to go at this all alone." Or they might say, "That guy was a total nut." However, if they wish to follow in my footsteps I have provided the way.

This Journal was not meant for everybody, but I do have some dear friends and family who wanted me to send them photos and updates of my trip. I did not have time to keep up with everyone's needs, so I just sent them all emails of what I was sending to my grandkids. My family and friends liked the stories so much that they encouraged me to make my Journal available to everyone, even you. In a short two week trip I rode through nine states and logged in around 3,700 miles. This is equivalent to a ride from California across the United States through to New York City and up to Sudbury, Canada. A few years ago I zigzagged across the United States from California to New York City and back, putting over 10,000 miles on the bike.

That was a 30 day ordeal with a lot more luggage and no computer, but it gave me the confidence to do this write-up and chronicle the events from a different perspective! My adventures were more intense as you can well imagine, however I did tape the adventures of my trip and I am slowly but surely putting it to print. That trip is a work in progress and I do a little here and there; I have all the receipts and can put the whole thing together like a puzzle, but you know how it is, life gets in the way, and things get put off. I am thinking, "Someday?"

—◆—

I bet you are wondering how I came by the name "PorkChop?" According to legend, there was this famous Harley Davidson bike racer that upon winning the race, he would do his victory lap with his little pet pig on his lap and people would yell "Hey, look at that Hog." Well the name stuck and from that point on people would always call a Harley Motorcycle a Hog. So when I bought my Harley many years ago we decided to name my bike "PorkChop."

I hope you enjoy the stories.

TABLE OF CONTENTS

ACKNOWLEDGMENTS

I would like to gratefully acknowledge my family and friends who encouraged me to write this book. Special thanks go to Alice Rivera a very dear friend who was instrumental in helping me with the Book. In addition, I give thanks to my children Joey, Michael, and Candi. And my brothers Manuel, Fons, and Gilbert. And let's not forget my dear friends who also helped prod me along. Alan Yelensky, Terry Ballantyne, Jan, Peggy, Melissa, Joan, RoseMary, Sherril, Angie, Carol, and Vikki. All of whom would have beaten me to a pulp had I not finished the book.

"Hey! Let's get together and go to Sturgis." I had heard it a hundred times. Then the excuses started, and one by one they chickened out when it was time to hit the road, so I decided I was not going to wait any longer. Life is just too damn short. If you're going to accomplish something the time to do it is NOW! Just "get out and do it!" (See Photo)

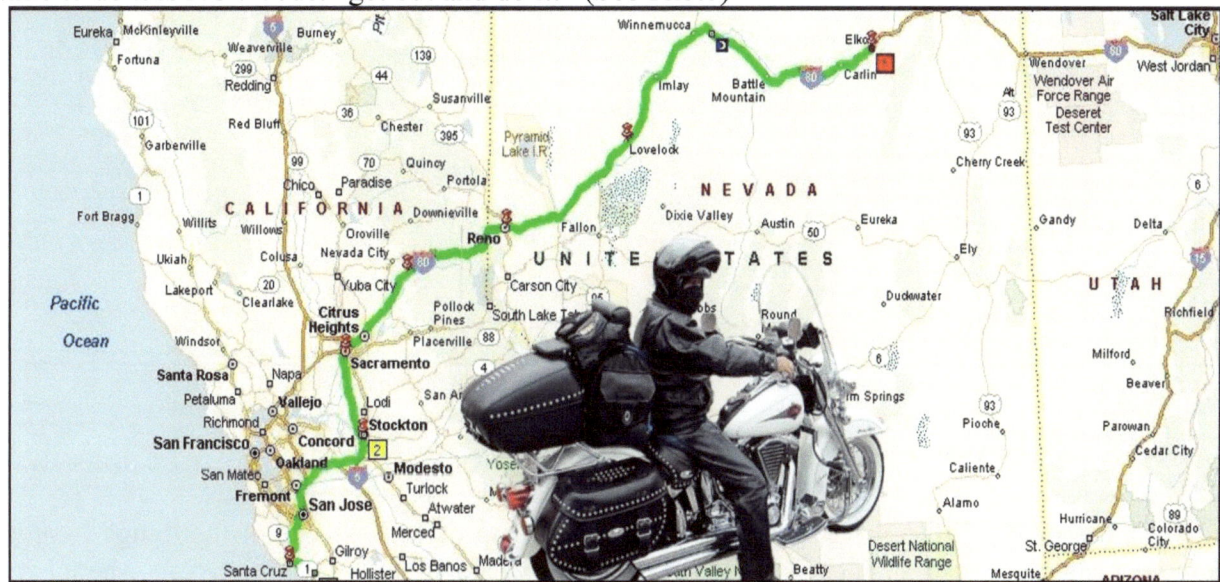

Watsonville, California to Elko, Nevada.

Day One … Me and PorkChop Bound For Sturgis

Watsonville, California is a sleepy little agricultural town about a two hour drive south of San Francisco and is nestled on the coast of the Monterey Bay. I left about 7:00 A.M. and headed N.E. to Sacramento, California. I fed PorkChop his chow in a nice Sacramento gas station and we picked up I-80 East to Reno, Nevada, then headed out to our first stop Elko, Nevada.

We traveled hard all day and got to Elko about 8:00 P.M. Needless to say it was a grueling 13-hour ride, non-stop, except for gas for PorkChop and a power bar for me. From Reno to Elko is the most barren desert you can imagine; you could land a flying saucer out there and no one would see it.

I was so tired when I checked into my hotel, I couldn't think clearly and when I tried to write a few paragraphs the sentences did not make sense, so I went to bed.

Ahhhh, Life is an Adventure.

Yours Always,
Joe

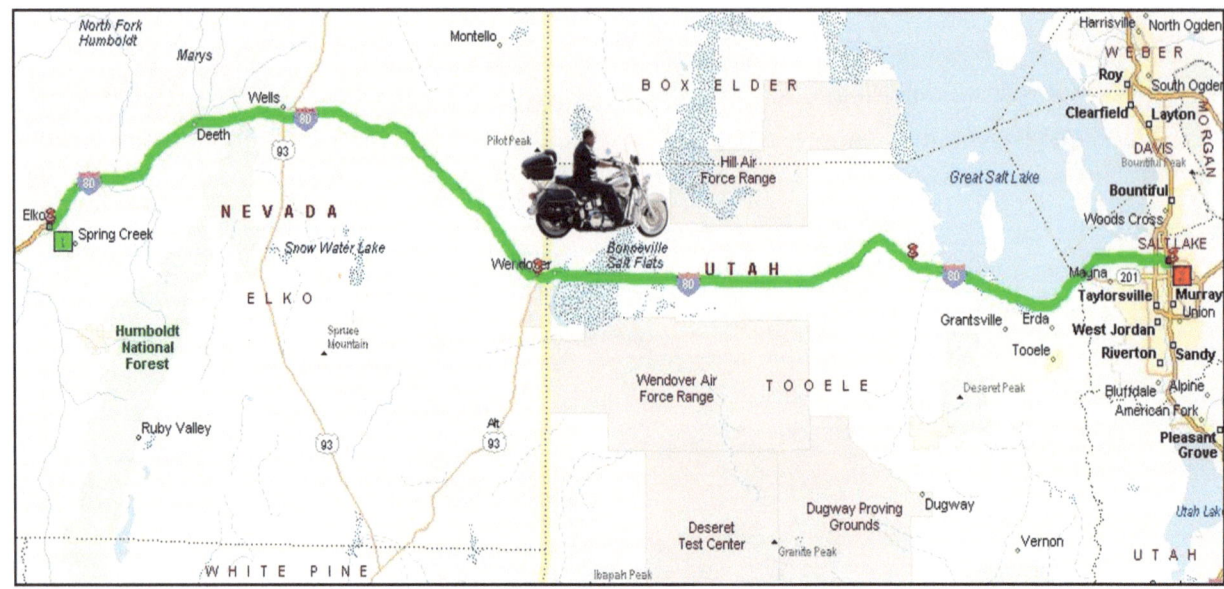

Elko, Nevada to Salt Lake City, Utah

Day Two … It's Heading My Way

It is morning in Elko; I just got up and grabbed a cup of coffee. One of the things I enjoy doing while sipping my cup of coffee is to read about the history and points of interests where I am staying. I shall try to pass on that information during my travels. For example; *Elko, Nevada: the first recorded white man in the Elko area was a fur trapper by the name of Peter Skene Ogden. In 1827, supposedly, the name Elko was derived from an Elk and later an "o" was added to ease the pronunciation and thus the name Elko. Elko is the fourth largest county in the United States consisting of 17,181 square miles, as big as five of the New England states plus the District of Columbia.*

Well here I am and I have not decided which way I am going or where I am going next. What a liberating feeling.

No Agenda!
No Expectation!
No Pressures!
Just me and the road!

There are things to see and people to meet. All I know is that I am going to mount my iron horse and ride off into the rising sun. I am going where I have never been before . . . to explore and seek new places and meet and mingle with the natives. I have enclosed a picture of me starting out on my new adventure. There will be more to follow; as soon as I figure out where I am going next.

I got a late start today which proved to be a very bad idea. I left Elko, Nevada for Salt Lake City, Utah which is normally a three to four hour trip. (See Map) As I settled myself on PorkChop, I felt the sun on my neck and something told me leaving at 11:00 was a bad idea.

As a long time pilot, I know not to fly my plane over the desert in the afternoon and to that list of prohibitions I have now added a motorcycle. It was already very hot, and I could hardly sit on the saddle, but I knew I had to hit the road and get the hell out of Dodge.

As I took off down the highway, the wind was hitting me from all directions. First a headwind, then out of nowhere I get side swiped, practically knocking me off my iron horse. PorkChop is a changeling and under 50 miles an hour he is the Porker, but over 50 he becomes "White Lightning." He is then my fast and dependable Iron Horse. There are dust devils and dirt whirling all around me and I get sand blasted. It's so bad that I can hardly see the road, and it's non-stop for hours. The sandy dust is in my teeth, filling up my ears, and collecting in every crevice of my face. It is a miserable, dry feeling made worse by lack of visibility. "Will this ever end?" my mind is screaming.

This is truly 'God forsaken Territory.' Who could live out here? I see no sign of life anywhere for hundreds of miles when suddenly, off in the horizon I see a great giant lake, "Oh, it must be Salt Lake City," I say to Pork, anticipating an end to my agony. "No such luck!" I soon find out by the signs up ahead that Salt Lake City is still hundreds of miles ahead. Now I see it's the Bonneville Salt Flats, "WOW!!" lots of history here: *In 1833, trapper and legendary frontiersman, Joseph R. Walker named the area after his employer, Captain Benjamin L. E. Bonneville. In 1846, the ill-fated Donner-Reed party while crossing the Salt Flats were slowed down and mired in the mud, which was a contributing factor in the tragedy that befell them in the Sierra Nevada's. In addition, in the 1930s, Ab Jenkins began setting endurance speed records at Bonneville. Since that time the Bonneville Salt Flats have attracted racers from throughout the world and have become the site of numerous land speed records. Bonneville issues over 20 commercial film permits a year.*

I tell Pork that a great movie was made here named, "The Worlds' Fastest Indian," starring Anthony Hopkins.

Suddenly I have this strong urge to give my iron horse the spurs and give it full throttle and off we go … 70, now 80, now 90 and 100 and up to 110 mph. Now I see telephone poles flying by me in a blur and I am praying to God, "Please Lord, if I hit the pavement do not let me live through it." I do not want to survive a hit like this. There would be nothing left of me to pick up. Suddenly out of nowhere I get lifted and picked up by a wind shear and dropped on the side of the road. I am thinking, "WOW!!" "that's a message, as I pull back on the reins." Now I am only doing 90 and that feels real slow. As I look at the telephone poles flying by, I glance out into the desert beyond them. My thoughts go out to the men and women who made this trip on slow moving wagon trains in this miserable heat. They certainly were strong and resilient people. I am suddenly filled with appreciation for what they did. We should all be very proud of their accomplishments. At my speed, it only takes a few minutes for me to travel distances that took them hours and hours. Plus they pulled livestock, ate dried food along the way and had no sanitation or showers.

I am now doing 90 most of the time and feeling okay with that speed. I do however, constantly keep an eye out for Smokey the Bandit. I really do not want to get a ticket. That's all I need. Boy, when you get hit by a bug at these speeds, it feels like a bullet just hit you and it really hurts. What? What in the hell is that looming ahead?

It's headed our way!

If things were not bad enough with the desert and the dust and now I am heading right into a thunderstorm. I see four or five of them and I am caught right out here in the middle of the desert with no place to hide or duck for cover. There is lightning flashing all around me; what to do? Only thing to do is hit the spurs and try to outrun it. 95, now 100, and now 110 again, and still that damn storm is catching up to me and there is another one straight ahead of me, what to do? Wait, there is a bridge straight ahead of me. Great I can hide under it and wait it out. WAIT IT OUT!!!! Hell no, not me!! Into the mouth of the storm we ride, lightning flashing all around me . . . then I see the first drop on the windshield, then another, then out of nowhere mother nature decides to punish me and lets loose with torrents of water, an experience I had never felt in my life.

I feel like I am getting stung by bees, but it's not bees, its bits of hail and I hear ping--ping--ping all around me hitting the bike. "Damn it! What have I gotten myself into?" I am totally soaked from head to toe and I am almost leaning 90 degrees just to keep from being knocked over by the wind. Suddenly, after what seemed like hours, I get through the storm and now I am on the other side of it. Thank God I made it. Then BOOM! I am hit with another one. OH MY GOD NOT ANOTHER ONE! A minute of relief and then I'm hit again and again. I not only went through one hell of a thunderstorm, but I got hit with five of them as you can see by the picture.

As I start to slow down and apply the brakes it feels like my foot weighs a ton. What the heck? I can hardly move my right leg when I suddenly find that my pant leg has blown up and my right boot was completely full of water and was spilling out of the boot. Damn!!

A half hour later I pull into Salt Lake City. Had the storm been delayed just a half hour longer I would have made it to Salt Lake high and dry. Oh well, story of my life. Now my main goal when I got there was to go to a Harley Davidson dealership and buy a tee shirt with Harley Davidson Utah on it. So, I called them to ask for directions. They told me that they were closing at 5:00 P.M. So, I moseyed on up and got there about 4:10 P.M. They were closing up shop and they would not sell me a tee shirt because the registers were all closed. I raised holy hell and told them I rode all the way from California just to get a shirt, but they didn't seem to care.

I finally broke down and begged and told them I would pay extra just to get the damn shirt, they still didn't care. I banged on the door and waved money at them. Finally they let me in and I got my shirt. Nobody has ever said I was a doormat!

OK, that's done, now let's find a place to bed down. I found a Ramada Inn, parked PorkChop who looked like hell from all the rain, and unloaded him. I eat apples and power bars along the way, but it is my ritual that at the end of my day, I will treat myself to a very nice steak dinner with a nice glass of wine. If lobster is available, then I will have that, but I will have something wonderful to celebrate my making it through the day, alive and on two wheels.

As I settled in for the night I made myself a promise that I would not get a late start and deal with late afternoon desert winds again so I set the clock for 6:30 A.M. There, that should do it. I was not planning on staying here overnight but after doing battle with Mother Nature I felt my iron horse and I needed to bed down for the night.

Well Good Night.

Yours Always,
Joe

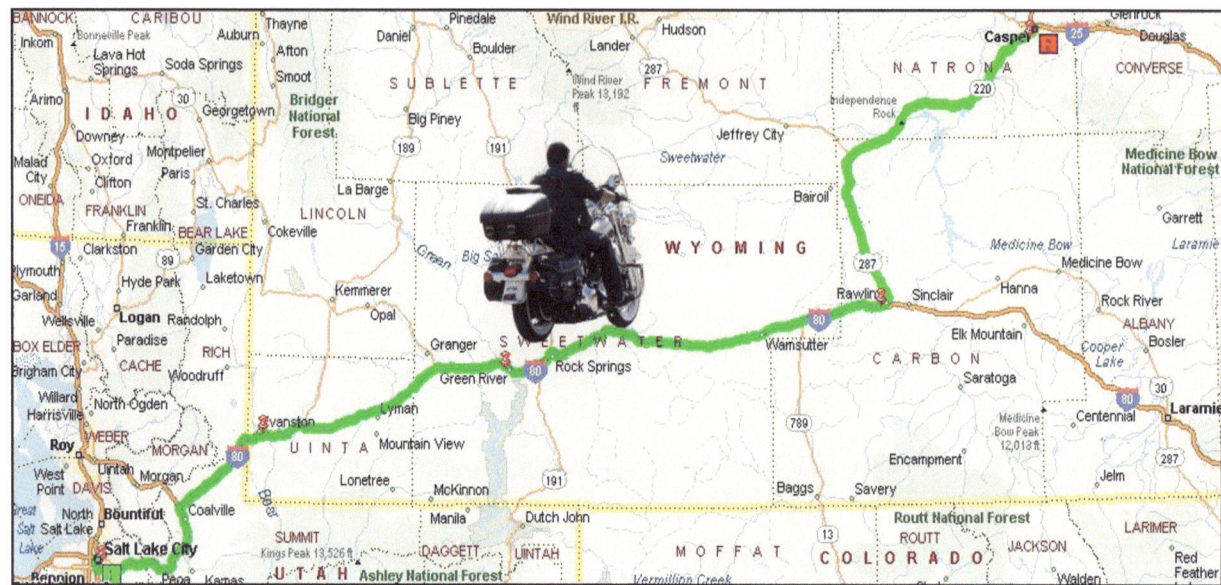

Salt Lake City, Utah to Casper, Wyoming

Day Three . . . In To the Storm We Ride

Well I woke up at 6:30 A.M., grabbed a cup of coffee and read up on this place, it seems that: *Salt Lake City was founded on July 24, 1847, by a group of Mormon pioneers. The pioneers, led by Brigham Young, were the first non-Indians to settle permanently in the Salt Lake Valley. The founding group numbered 148, consisting of 143 men, three women, and two children. The Mormons came to the valley in search of a region where they could practice their religion, "free from hostile mobs and persecution." When Brigham Young first saw the valley he said, "This is the right place." Construction on the Mormon temple began in 1853, but the capstone of this magnificent structure was not put into place until 1892.*

After I finished my cup of coffee, I decided to take a shower. When I started to get dressed I found that my leathers were still soaked! I had one hell of a time putting them on. Have you ever tried to put on wet leathers? It's not fun nor easy. I strained and pulled and shivered into those heavy damp things. Can you believe it? I recently bought a top-of-the line rain gear just for this kind of occasion and I did not bring it with me. I thought about it but I just did not have room in my saddlebags, plus I did not think I was going to get caught up in heavy storms. Oh well, it's all part of the adventure. I figured they will eventually dry as we travel, so I grabbed a bite to eat, loaded up Pork and by now it's 10:30 A.M.!

What the hell is wrong with me? I don't know what in the world takes me so long. Anyhow, I decided I would not leave Salt Lake without taking a picture of The Mormon Temple. (See Photo)

Mormon Temple and Pork   **Temple in background**

I rode into town and damn it, I could not find it. Honest to God. I must have asked over a dozen people, where is it? And no one knew. I could not believe it!! I thought these people were all Mormons and they should all know where it was, but noooooooo.

Finally, I saw a moving van and I thought I would ask the driver if he knew where it was. He would have to know, after all the building is downtown. And yes, he knew, it was just around the corner, but you can't see it any longer. They have walled it in and there are all these buildings all around it now. Needless to say, it was a real nightmare, so I took my pictures and went on my way.

I finally got on Hwy 80 and headed East (See Map) and gave it full throttle. It is now 12:15 P.M. way later than my start from my previous day. What happened to my great laid out plan on getting an early start?

I am now in this God forsaken prairie and the winds are already knocking me around. Teaches me right, I deserve to get the hell beat out of me. Hey wait, I have been a good boy, I don't deserve this. I get hit from all sides by nasty headwinds. I am holding on for dear life and my knuckles are turning white from hanging on so tight. Sometimes I lean over so much just to stay on the highway that I feel like those bike racers that race around the track and drag their knees on the pavement.

Finally, up ahead I see a sign that says welcome to Wyoming, so I stop for a photo. Just as I am taking the photo it starts to pour and it comes down in buckets for just a spell, but enough to get me and PorkChop good and wet. Of course the roads are now all wet and slippery. What else is new? (See Photo)

Wyoming here we come

While I am taking my photo, old Pork starts squealing like a pig, saying that he is hungry. I said "OK! OK!" A little later I noticed a little town named Evanston. (See Map) So I stopped and gave the Porker his chow, while I was munching on an apple I checked my tires to see if I was wearing out the treads on the sides, since I had been leaning so much.

Hey, last night while I was lying in bed I thought, "You know, I am like the Lone Ranger, (the guy on TV) because I am the Lone Rider." I usually make these rides by myself and since he called his horse Silver, I think I will name my Iron Horse, Silver, so Silver it is. Anyhow I give the spurs to Silver, first 70, then 80, then 90. Silver seems to like 90. So we maintain 90 for a long while. All of sudden, I start to see Smokey all around me, it seems that every 5 or 6 miles Smokey has pulled some poor soul over and I can see them crying, begging for forgiveness. Of course the cops won't give them a break, so I decided that it was best to pull the reins on Silver and slow it down to 80 and keep an eye out. Anyhow, it's boring prairie as far as you can see. (See Photo)

Endless miles of asphalt

All I see is a strip of asphalt for hundreds and hundreds of miles until it disappears into the horizon. I give it full throttle and Silver and I are once again at 90. It seems like it took forever as we climbed the plateau thinking the end is in sight, but noooooo. We have more miles of asphalt that never seem to end. This goes on for hours and hours and all the while I get the hell beat out of me by the wind. Who in the hell would live out here? Only prairie dogs I guess.

Looks like Silver is starving for hay, better pull in and get him some food and me too! I pull into a little town named Green River (See Map) and he gets fed while I have an apple. While I am standing there eating my apple, (See Photo) a nice looking lady comes out of the store, walks over and gives me a big hug, and says, "Welcome to Wyoming." She starts to tell me about her little town and how her husband works in the mines and about her kids and so on. Then she bids me adios and says, "have a nice ride." I'm thinking, "WOW!! What a nice little town this is, everyone here is so friendly." I waved goodbye to her as she drove off and I turned around and finished feeding Pork his slop.

My apple a day

I mounted up and hit the starter and Pork started to cough, sneeze, spit and choke. He decided to throw a tantrum and wouldn't start. Damn it Pork! What the hell is the matter with you? I tried several more times to get him going, but he was being stubborn. (See Photo)

Pork throwing a tantrum. . . . Bad Pig!!!

I finally pushed and heaved him over to the side so that other people could get gas for their vehicles. I decided to get off of him and go into the store to cool off as I was so mad I could have kicked him, but I didn't. After about ten minutes I came out of the store and went up to him and started to talk real nice to him like, "PAAALLEESE, Pork PAAALLLEESE start," as I am rubbing his nose (front fender). I mounted up, hit the start button and he decided to start. I guess he liked all the gooey sweet talk I laid on him. (Photo) Well, now we start to merge onto the freeway and hit the trail once more. Within a short time the winds start to beat the hell out of me again. All of a

The Beasts are coming

sudden, the road turns into a one-lane road, construction work I guess. So now I have giant semi-trucks (I call them enormous beasts). (See Photo)

They fly by with nothing but a whisper of yellow paint between me and instant death. The force of the air as it moves past me is like being hit by a 155-mile blast of wind right on my chest. The Beasts are moving at 75 miles an hour and I am riding up on them at 90. The atmospherics are staggering. As I pass truck after truck, I am hit with enormous blasts of wind again and again; this goes on and on, as it batters me for hours and hours. I count over 500 semi-trucks in one hour. I finally gave up as I was getting sleepy, you know, like counting sheep.

Finally, the construction ends and we are a divided road again. Thank God, I could not have taken this much longer. I was exhausted after all of that. I looked around me, and all I see is miles and miles of open prairie (See Photo) and an endless streak of asphalt as far as the eye can see.

Miles of openness

Do I have enough fuel to make it? That has plagued me this whole trip as I only carry 5 gallons, and the stations are so few and far between that I have sweated bullets many times. On this trip I have ridden on fumes, always hoping to make it to the next gas station. As soon as I can, I am going to buy a rubber hose just in case I run out of fuel out here in no-man's land.

OH NO!! Not again. What's this I see; another storm? It's fast approaching and is heading right for me; damn! not again, PLEASE NOT AGAIN!!!(See Photo)

It's coming this way

I have nowhere to hide or duck for cover. Thank God it's going right past to the right of me. I am safe, finally a break. A few minutes later I feel water on the back of my neck. What's going on? There is blue sky all around me. I look straight up, and here is this big black cloud, right on top of my head. No, no, no, I just had a shower this morning, I don't need another one PLEASE!! That damn storm went right past me on the right. Then came right behind me, and just drenched me. I could not outrun it as there were trucks in front of me and it was a no passing lane. Sometimes you just can't win. Needless to say I got drenched. All of a sudden I get hit with a bullet on my right hand and on my thigh. Damn! It hurts and stings for a long time. Bugs, and at this speed, it hurts like hell.

Finally, way out on the horizon I see a speck. It looks like a town and it must be Rawlins, Wyoming. (See Map) I look at the tank and it is on fumes. It's always a sickening feeling not knowing for sure if I can make it. I am now completely empty and just made it this time. I feed PorkChop his chow, and he does not like it and starts choking and sputter won't start. Now what do I do? Damn Pig! I assume it's bad gas.

I wait awhile and let him cool down, and finally, PorkChop decides to start. I mount up and hit the trail once more. The Pork keeps belching and belching; threatening to quit. He finally stops belching so I gently open the throttle and we move along at a very slow pace until Silver kicks in and we are back to 90 again. I aim my iron horse north, and as I ride along, I notice that the terrain starts to look real pretty. Hey, I am really enjoying the ride now. This is what it's all about!! An hour and a half later, we arrive at Casper, Wyoming. (See Photo)

Casper, Wyoming

It was a seven-hour non-stop ride, so I checked into the first motel I saw. I unloaded the Pork, took a nice hot shower and went out looking for the nicest restaurant I could find. After treating myself to a nice dinner and a good glass of wine, I mosey on back to the motel and hit the sack.

Yours Always,
Joe

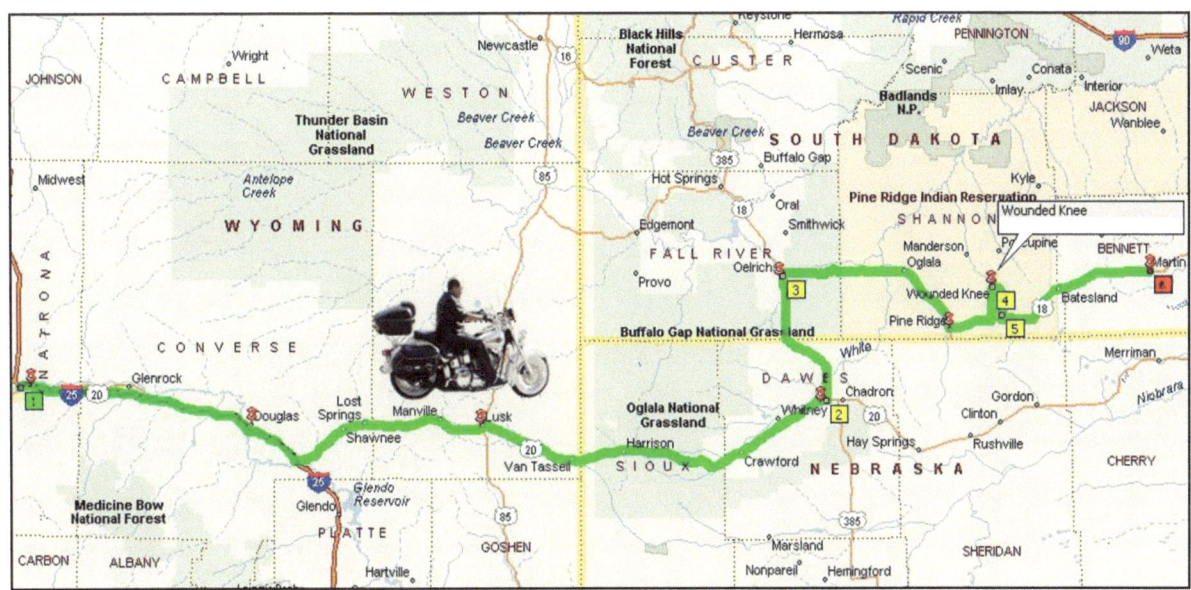

Casper, Wyoming to Martin, South Dakota

Day Four . . . Wounded Knee

I woke up sore and tired as usual, while sipping on my coffee I looked up the history of Casper: It seems that: *The city of Casper was established in 1888 and named after a young Lieutenant, Caspar Collins, who was sent to provide safe escort for a wagon train carrying critical supplies for the fort. Soon after he crossed the bridge, he and his command of twenty-five men ran into Red Cloud and thousands of Lakota warriors. The soldiers retreated across the bridge in hand-to-hand combat; although all were wounded, most of them made it to safety. Collins didn't. In an attempt to put a wounded man back onto his horse, he lost control of his mount which galloped directly into the Lakota force. According to survivor accounts, Collins had an arrow sticking out of his forehead, the reins in his teeth, and a pistol in each hand. His body was found several days later with twenty-four arrows in it.*

You just never know about these towns you visit until you take the time to read up on them. Well, time to get going. I took a shower, packed up Pork, and hit the road. I looked at my watch, damn! Another late start. Oh well, better than yesterday, it is now 10:00 A.M. I can't help but wonder, "What the hell takes me so long?"

I get outside and guess what? No wind, "WOW!!" This is great, this is the way it should be, as I mount up and we hit the trail. We are now picking up speed and Pork has changed into my iron horse, Silver. Now we are at 70, now 80, and finally 90. Silver likes it there. Looking out onto the horizon, I see nothing but prairie and more prairie, (See Photo)

Endless road

 and miles and miles of endless asphalt that disappears over the hill and merges into the sky. This goes on and on for hours.

I have been on the road for hours now and its getting really, really hot, what gives? Oh, I see, no wind. So now it's hotter than hell and I am going to get cooked out here!! Now I find myself begging PAALLEASE!! I want wind or better yet, a little rain shower would sure be nice right about now. Hey Pork, I see a dark rain cloud on the horizon, so I give Silver the spurs and we leap up to 95. Now we have become storm chasers instead of running away like we did before. WAIT!! That damn cloud is moving away from us and is now passing on our right side . . . NOOOOOO! Please just a little bit of rain is all I am asking, just to cool off. No such luck, Mother Nature is punishing me for yelling and telling her off yesterday. No cooling off for you she says.

Man you can't win. I finally decide to get off Silver and take a swig of water from my canteen and I think, "Maybe I can do a little rain dance or pray to the rain gods," as I am yelling, "PLEASSSSSE just a little bit of cool rain would sure be nice." I am not asking for much, but noooo. Oh well, enough begging. I mount up and give Silver the spurs. Off we go slowly moving up to 90 again watching miles and miles of prairie and asphalt disappearing behind me.

After about one hour, I see a car coming toward me with his lights blinking like mad. "Hmmmm, I wonder what the heck that's all about." When all of a sudden it hits me, "Damn!" It's a warning, a cop is ahead. I pull on the reins and Silver slows to a crawl just as I see Smokey hiding behind some trees. Thank God, for the warning from the motorist, I would have been nailed for sure. Once we passed the cop, I hit the throttle and we hit 90 again.

After miles of hard riding, I start to smell rubber and I am thinking, "What is wrong with Pork?" Just then, I look ahead of me and see I am behind a big semi-truck. I notice that one of his back tires is wobbling like crazy… it's his recap, and it is ready to fly off. If I get hit by the flying rubber I am a dead man for sure!! I give Silver full throttle and I pull hard left, pulling right up to the truck's door, as I am honking my horn and pointed to his tires, he got the message and started to pull off to the side of the road.

After riding for a spell, I see Silver is hungry, so I pull off into a little town named, Douglas. (See Map) I dismounted, fed Pork his chow, rested a bit, ate an apple, took a drink from my canteen, mounted up and hit the trail again. After another hour and a half of riding, I go through this little town named, Lusk. (See Map) To be on the safe side I decided to get some gas. As I pulled into town I noticed a group of riders in line waiting to gas up, who were also making their way to Sturgis. (See Photo)

The line up

17

Nebraska here we come

Pork and I waited our turn, gassed up and hit the trail once more. I did not bother to B.S. with any of them as they were doing enough of that on their own. After many more miles of riding I see a sign that says Nebraska. (See Photo)

As I am taking the photo and look toward the horizon, I notice that I'm losing the sunshine and it's starting to get gray. I mount up and give Silver the spurs and off we go. Within a short time I noticed in the distance a rain cloud. WONDERFUL!! Mother Nature changed her mind, I am going to get some relief here. However, as I get closer and closer the cloud gets bigger and bigger and darker and darker. WAIT!!! I just wanted a little shower, not to get drenched in a storm, but noooooo. Here it comes and I mean I get totally soaked. It rained on me for more than three hours straight. There was nothing I could do but just keep riding. If I pull over every time it rains, I will never reach my destination. I am soaking wet and it is still pouring. I think I overdid my rain dance and prayer.

Anyhow, it is still pouring rain and I am totally drenched. Soon I see a sign that says Chadron and Hwy 385 (See Map). I pull hard to the left and head into South Dakota, Indian territory. After riding for almost three hours in the rain non-stop, Pork starts squealing that he is hungry again so I pull into a gas station at a little crossroads named Oelrichs (See Map) and I tell one of the Indians that I plan to go through the Badlands and on to see Custer's Last Stand.

He tells me that if I take this certain road, which he points out, I could cut across and save some time. It is still raining, but I have no choice. I take his advice and move slowly down the road. After about a half hour of avoiding water filled pot holes on the road, I come to a sign that says BUMP! (See Photo)

Miles of mud and slime

I look ahead and I see nothing but a muddy dirt road. What do they mean by bump? It looks like this is the end of the road. I stop and get off Pork to take a better look. As I walk up to the road, I see to my horror that this is the end and there is no more paved road. All I can see for miles is a muddy, soaked, deeply entrenched trail that has very deep ruts. It's menacing looking and it looks very ugly as it is still raining. It also looks very slippery. I can't go back. There was no place to stay the way I came. I have no choice but to go forward.

But how? These ruts are very deep and I don't think we can navigate through them safely. What to do? But wait! I see that at the extreme right side of the road the vehicles have not torn up that part of it so I am thinking, "I can ride along the extreme right side and stay on that hard part of the dirt road."

As I climb up on Pork and we gently move on to the right hard part of the road, I realized immediately that we were screwed. It was an illusion, it looked like it was hard but the moment we waded into it we sank into deep, deep slimy mud. Imagine this as quicksand; it looks hard on top but the moment you step on top of it, it gives way and you get swallowed up. The only thing that kept us from going deeper into the mud was Pork's foot rest which acted like little side boards. I immediately put both my feet onto the side of the bike and my boots sank deep into the mud. That prevented us from falling over to the side. I was totally committed at this point and I was forced to go forward; there is no reverse, and I could not turn the wheel to go back even if I wanted to.

I gave it full throttle and we slipped and slid forward all the time throwing mud out the back of the bike like one of those water jet skis. I realized right away that I had to move out of this quicksand and get into the middle of the road where those deep ruts were. However, I was having a very difficult time just trying to move the front tire. I slowly but surely, inch by inch, moved to the center of the road. It was a long, slow process which had to be done with extreme care for fear of dropping the bike. I kept giving it full throttle and helped it along by pushing with my feet. I soon realized that I was also having a difficult time pulling my boots out of the mud. There was one point when I thought for sure I was going to lose my boot which got stuck in the mud.

We finally got to the middle of the road and now we faced another problem. The foot rests which acted like little side boards and kept us from sinking deeper into the quicksand was now blocking us from moving forward. We were so deep into the trench that now when I wanted to go forward the foot pegs were stopping us. All I could do was give it full throttle and push real hard with my feet, causing the foot pegs to slice thru the mud. Luckily the mud was wet and slimy and soft which allowed us to move forward very slowly. This misery went on for miles as I am crawling along this muddy trail at about one mile an hour, constantly keeping both feet hanging over the side trying to keep Pork right side up. I am praying and cursing, all at the same time. "WOE--IS!--ME--WOE--IS!--ME!"

I was very nervous and extremely concerned that I would drop the bike to one side or the other, and there was no way in hell that I could ever pick Pork up in this slippery, slimy mess. "He is one very fat Pig." Plus, I had not seen any cars come by the whole time we were engulfed in this slimy mud pit.

I guess the locals knew better than to come down this road. As we moved forward inch by inch, it seemed to me like it took hours. As I pushed and pushed and pushed, I finally saw way off in the distance what appeared to be solid road. It gave me a glimmer of hope and renewed strength to keep on pushing. I was so tired and my boots were so deep into mud that it took all my strength just to pull my legs and the boots out of the mud.

After an hour or more of this snail's pace, I reached asphalt again. "THANK GOD, I MADE IT!!" I think out loud. I was never so happy in all my life to see asphalt. I felt like dropping to my knees and kissing the road, which I didn't by the way! But I wanted to! When I got Pork onto the asphalt, I dropped the kick stand, and turned the motor off. I just sat there on the bike and let the rain fall on me, I didn't care. Matter of fact I welcomed the rain, I figured it would wash the mud off my jacket, chaps, and boots.

After resting a while I decided to hit the trail once again. I started Porker and slowly moved on to the road when all of a sudden PorkChop starts to squeal like the pig that he is, but it is a horrible sounding squeal, something I had not heard before. I get off the bike and check to see what the hell he is squealing about. It's then that I noticed that the tires and fenders are full of and caked with mud. So, I get on my knees and start to dig the mud out with my bare hands. I bet that Indian is laughing like hell. He got even with the "White Man" after all. "Ha-Ha-Ha," he is saying. Oh well, this is all part of my Great Adventure. After more than two hours since my last gas stop, and all that fighting through the mud, I stop at a little town called Pine Ridge. There is a lot of history here, so I pull in and feed the Pork his usual slop. I am sopping wet and I do not even feel like eating, I just want a hot cup of coffee. As I am sipping my java, I decide I'd better just get a motel room, stay here and get out of this rain. I asked a local Indian where I could find a motel nearby. He says, "You'll need to go back 27 miles the way you came or go down this road to a town called Martin, they have lots of motels there." Then, he added, "You really should get out of this rain, you're heading right into a storm and the winds can get up to 90 miles per hour around these parts."

Well I will be damned if I am going to backtrack 27 miles. After leaving Pine Ridge, it was very slow moving due to the heavy rains. Slowly but surely, we started to encounter the storm that the Indian had warned us about. I was now starting to feel the headwinds. They were getting stronger and stronger as I proceeded into the storm. It was so bad that I was having a difficult time maintaining the bike and keeping it upright. In addition to that, the rain was now so relentless and so heavy, that I had to flip the visor up on my helmet in order to see the road. The moment I did that I felt stinging needles, which were heavy raindrops hitting my face. The rain was coming down so hard that I could see it bouncing two inches off the asphalt. At one point I could not see beyond my windshield. All of a sudden I felt the bike kind of glide under me and I could not feel the tires on the road any longer. At that point I knew I was hydroplaning, meaning that I was literally riding on a very, very thin sheet of water. I knew then, that it was a big "WAKE UP CALL." I slowly let up on the throttle, gingerly pulled to the side of the road, and came to a complete stop.

I then dropped the kickstand and just sat there with the engine running for fear that if I turned it off I might not be able to start it again. I sat there and sat there for what seemed like an eternity while the rain just continued its onslaught, never letting up for a minute. I couldn't do anything, there was no place to seek cover. All I could do was just sit there and take it. Besides, even if I could see shelter I could not move or ride to it for the fear that the bike would slide from under me and I would certainly get run over by the traffic as visibility was so bad they would not be able to see me in time. Mother Nature was saying, "You wanted rain, well I am giving you rain, how do you like that?" As I am shouting, "WHY ME? – WHY ME?"

Every once in a while, a car would go by, and the folks in the car would stare at me through the window. I am sure they were saying, "Oh look at the poor nut sitting out there in the cold and rain." Or, they might be saying, "Look at the stupid idiot!" More than likely it was the latter.

While sitting there exposed to the rain and wind, I could feel my leathers getting heavier and heavier and I was literally getting soaked to the bone. I was getting cold and starting to shiver, I knew when I got going again that it would be worse. When you add the wind chill factor, I knew I would become more miserable than I am now. Imagine if you will, having a heavy leather glove and sticking it into a bucket of water, how heavy that would be and how uncomfortable that would make you feel; that's how I felt over my whole body. Now, I could feel the cold water penetrating the leathers onto my bare skin, "WHAT A BUMMER!"

And of course since I had to leave the engine running while waiting out the storm, old Pork started in on me and how much he hated this whole adventure thing: That he is soooo sick and tired of all the rain, how he wants to go home to his pig pen, and how he hates to get wet. The only thing he liked about this whole trip was the mud and slime we encountered a few hours ago, etc., etc. "LORDY!--LORDY!--LORDY!" Now I have to listen to his crap. I finally told him to shut up and that I did not like this anymore than he did. Quite honestly, I was starting to think. "What in the hell am I doing out here? I want to go home too." But that was just a slight afterthought. I am the type of guy, that once I start something, I see it through to the end. That is just my style.

Finally, the rain started to subside. It did not stop raining, but I felt it was safe enough to go ahead because I could feel the road under me again. As I grabbed and squeezed the clutch on the handlebars a stream of water poured from my glove, that is how wet and thoroughly soaked I was. As I moved my foot to the brake I could feel that my socks were all wet as well. Apparently, the rain had penetrated through my leather boots. As I slowly started to move on to the road, old Pork started to snort, sneeze, cough and as usual, he started to act up again, I guessed it was water in the carburetor. Anyhow he kept snorting and complaining the whole time and wanted to go home. He kept that up for miles and miles up the road. I thought for sure, he was going to quit on me, just to teach me a lesson. During this whole trip to Martin, Silver never showed up as I had to keep the speed under 50 mph, because of the continual rain. And of course Pork being the pig that he is, never relented in his abuse towards me, always on the verge of quitting. Finally up the road I see a sign that says Wounded Knee. (See Photo)

It's raining but we must go

The story of Wounded Knee is that: *The Sioux were told by Kicking Bear and Short Bull that by wearing "Ghost Shirts" the ghost dancing warriors would become immune to the white man's bullets and could openly defy the soldiers and white settlers, and bring back the old days of the big buffalo herds. The Indians were ordered to surrender their arms. During the excitement, Yellow Bird, a medicine man, walked among the braves blowing on an eagle bone whistle, inciting the warriors to action, declaring that the "Ghost Shirt" worn by the warriors would protect them from the soldier's bullets.*

A shot was fired, and all hell broke loose. The troops fired a deadly volley into the Council warriors, killing nearly half of them. A bloody hand-to-hand struggle followed, since the Indians were armed mostly with clubs, knives and revolvers. The Hotchkiss guns fired 2-pound explosive shells on the groups, indiscriminately killing warriors, women, children and their own disarming soldiers. Soldiers were killed by cross-fire of their comrades in this desperate engagement. Resulting in the killing of more men, women and children, causing the battle to be referred to as the "Wounded Knee Massacre".

One hour later, 146 Indian, women and children lay dead. The bodies of many were scattered along a distance of two miles from the scene of the encounter. Twenty soldiers were killed on the field, and sixteen later died of wounds Four days later, an Army detail gathered up the Indian dead and buried them in a common grave at the top of the hill northwest of here. A monument marks this grave. "Ghost Dancing" ended with this encounter. The Wounded Knee battlefield is the site of the last armed conflict between the Sioux Indians and the United States Army.

Even though it's pouring rain on me and I am running real late, I have to take this detour and see this sight. After all, that's why I am on this trip, to explore and see things I have never seen before, so off we go. The rain was heavy and visibility was very poor. I was looking for a huge building or a very large monument. Consequently, we missed the site and went many miles past. We finally gave up as we could not see any buildings or anything for miles ahead. So we turned around and headed back to the main road. After riding for many miles back the way we came, I finally noticed this landmark. (See Photo)

At the massacre

We stopped and took the picture and headed back to the main road. This little detour took me 35 miles out of my way, but what the hey, this is all part of the Adventure.

Man, it's getting real late and it's getting real dark and it's still raining on me. That mud trip really caused me a huge delay. After little more than an hour of riding in the storm I see a glimmer of light way in the distance, thank God, civilization at last.

I roll into this town called Martin. It's the smallest town I have ever seen. I was told, that there would be "lots of motels." Well mark another one for the Indians, they got me again. There is only one in this town that I can find and it's a real dump. However, right now I am thinking, 'any port in a storm.' I jumped off Pork and was making a mad dash for the door when I happened to look back to see Pork squealing his lungs out yelling, "Sure, leave me out here all alone in this cold and miserable raining night." I felt bad for him and yelled back, "I will take good care of you tomorrow and feed you some good slop."

I go inside to find a line of people, all waiting to get a room. As I walked into the lobby I was totally sopping wet, and everyone stopped talking and just stared at me standing there dripping wet. There was a line of people waiting to get a room to get out of the rain. So I walked to the back of the line and as I did so, people again were looking and staring at me as I was making some real funny squishing noises as I walked. Every time I took a step you could hear a squishing sound. It was very embarrassing, plus I noticed that people were giving me a lot of space.

I soon realized that I stunk. Have you ever smelled wet leather? It does not smell very nice. After a while this young man came up behind me with a mop and was following me. As I moved forward he would mop up the floor behind me. I am thinking, "I don't care if they charge $500 dollars a night I am staying here." Then I hear the clerk tell one of the customers, "I don't think we have any more rooms. Everyone wants to get out of the storm." My heart sank to the floor and I think, "Oh no, I am screwed. I will pay just to sit in the lobby and get out of the rain." At least those other people had cars they could sit in and wait out the storm. Not me though, I am sitting out there all exposed to the elements.

Once again I think Mother Nature is getting even with me for telling her off during the day. Finally, it's my turn to speak with the clerk and I am begging. "PLEASSSSE!" "I will sleep in the laundry room if I have to." She says, "You're in luck, this is our last room." Thank God, I needed a break.

All of a sudden, I had this sensation of relief, joy, peace, you know the feeling, and I was in seventh heaven as I hurriedly brought all my stuff into the room and dropped it on the floor. I could not wait to rip off the heavy wet leathers. However, I found it to be extremely difficult, as the leather was clinging to me like glue. I finally got them off and could not wait to take a hot shower and make myself a nice cup of hot tea. WHAT? NO COFFEE POT!!! Who doesn't put a coffee pot in the room!? Tom Bodett would never treat anyone like this. I jumped into a pair of sweats and ran down the hall to the clerk's desk, to tell the lady, "That there is no coffee pot in the room." She looks at me, as though to say, "What do you think this is, the Hilton?" There is no question in my mind that she was thinking exactly those words. "No. And by the way, there is no continental breakfast either." I sighed deeply "Oh well," I say to myself, "What do you expect from a flea-bitten motel?" I turn and find my way back to my room where I notice that there is only one thin towel, one face towel, and no soap. Luckily, I always have a bar of soap with me. Grumbling under my breath, I took a hot shower and settled in for the night.

Sometime during the night I woke up and realized that I was starting to itch all over my legs and arms. "Damn," I am thinking, "I am not alone in this bed! There are bed bugs in here, . . . I just know it." I am sure there are still some 'country bumpkins' who still bring their sheep, chickens, cows, and pigs in here with them. "Whoa!!" "Did I say pigs?" I'd best not let PorkChop overhear that comment or he probably won't start in the morning.

I just could not sleep during the night with all that rain and thunder right outside my window; it sounded like cannons were firing outside. Then there was the rain and wind banging on the windows, and of course, I was itching like crazy. Oh, what a night! At least tomorrow I have something to look forward to . . . the Badlands.

Good Night and Sweet Dreams,
Joe

P.S. Damn it!! Due to the rains, this trip took a little more than nine hours because of having to fight the mud and slime.

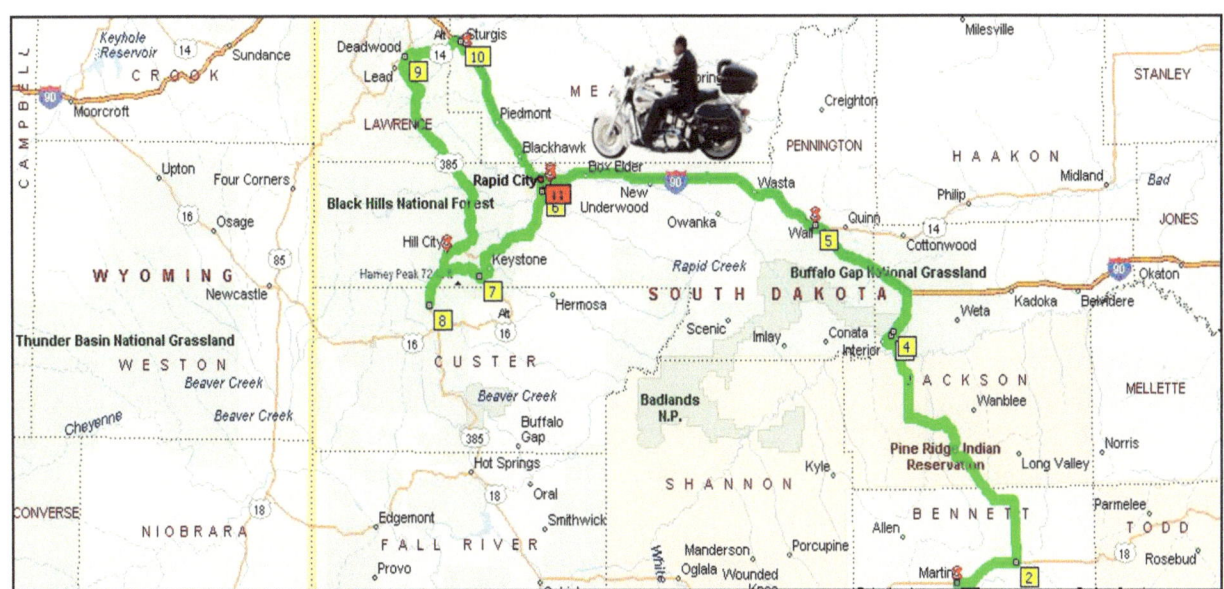

Martin, South Dakota to Rapid City, South Dakota

Day Five … The Badlands

Martin has a population of 1,106 and is surrounded on three sides by the Pine Ridge and Rosebud Sioux Indian Reservations, the town of Martin is a good base camp to experience the Lakota culture. To the north are the rugged Dakota Badlands and the moonscapes of the Badlands National Park. To the south are the Sandhills of Nebraska. Sandwiched in between are Martin and the flat lands used for wheat farming.

Well I got up at 7:00 A.M. as usual, but did not get my butt out of that miserable place until 10:30. I finally figured out what is taking me so long to get going. I have to unload Pork at the end of every day, then load him up again every morning. I don't want anyone going through the saddle bags, stealing things during the night.

Back to this morning . . . no coffee, no breakfast, nothing but a glass of water. The worst thing was yet to come though. You may remember that my leathers were soaking wet last night. Well this morning, my leathers were still damp. I could not zip up my jacket, because of the dampness, but I decided it would dry as soon as I hit the road. No problem. But then I tried to put my boots on, and damn if I didn't get stuck half way into my boot! Have you ever tried to put on high top boots when they are damp? So, there I was, with my foot stuck half way in, and I couldn't push it further into the boot, or pull my foot out. I got a leg cramp trying to push and pull my way into the boot. I had one foot without a boot and one leg stuck half way in. I was in pain trying to get out of the boot and was hopping all around the place. At one point, I considered calling the desk for help. . . . "HELP!!! I can't get out of my boot!" How stupid that would have sounded.

I am sure the locals would have talked about that for years, and that was enough to get me to try again and again. I finally pushed it in all the way. The other foot wasn't any easier but, I DID

IT! I finally mounted up and hit the road. *"On the road again, just can't wait to get on the road again. Seeing things that I may never see again I just can't wait to get on the road again." Sound familiar? Thanks Willie.

"OH MY GOD!!!" I can't believe it. What a beautiful day it is. There are crystal blue skies, as far as the eye can see, without a single cloud in the sky. "WOW!!" "Thank you Lord." This is what I am talking about!! I guess he gave me a few miserable days, just so I could really appreciate this awesome day. No wind, no heat, skies of blue and endless miles of winding curvy roads through beautiful valleys with lakes and grazing cattle. This is just absolutely gorgeous country. I am so happy and excited that I keep throwing my fist in the air and yelling "Yippy!" I'm screaming and howling, and just letting it all out! Man, oh man! This is what it's all about! I am one happy biker!! You have no idea how very happy and lucky I am to be riding these roads right now. If I die tomorrow, I will die a happy man! Well maybe not tomorrow . . . you know what I mean . . . heh-heh.

Feeling on top of the world, I give Silver the spurs. On we go, about 75 mph right now on these back country roads. I had better not go any faster on this curvy road. I am passing acres and acres of green land to my right, the deepest green you have ever seen . . . and wait! To my left, there are acres and acres of bright yellow fields as far as the eye can see. "What in the hell is that stuff?" I think as I pull on the reins. I slow to about 40. It was then I noticed them, sunflowers with their beautiful faces turned up to the sky. Now I know where all the sunflower seeds come from.

I grab a handful of throttle, and kick it up to 75 again, and settle in for the ride. I am just thoroughly enjoying the whole experience. I look at the road ahead and the asphalt just keeps on going all the way to the horizon. I am lost in this experience when all of a sudden, the road breaks hard left under me and I yell, "WHAT THE HELL!!!" I am leaning hard to the left to make the turn, but I can't make it!! I straighten the bike up, grab the brake handle, and hit the foot brake really hard and skid my way into the embankment. I am laying rubber as I finally come to a stop with my front tire hanging over the edge of the embankment. "DAMN, YOU STUPID IDIOT," I scream at myself. I immediately look behind me, to make sure no car is going to nail me from the back. I pull the bike back off the embankment, roll to a stop a few feet away, and dismount. I walk around the bike a few times, to shake off the jitters. That was a damn close call.

As I walk back to analyze the scene, I can now see what happened. It was some sort of a 3-D effect. I was looking straight ahead, and saw miles of open road, as I was so used to seeing. There was another road, however, just below the road that I was on. The second road, somehow, gave me the illusion that I would just keep going straight forever. There were no signs or arrows or anything indicating that the road was going to turn to the left. It suddenly just did, and it was a really sharp left turn. I'll bet there have been some accidents here, I thought to myself. Sure enough, as I looked down the embankment, I could see a lot of damage down below. I am sure that many autos have gone over the edge of this road at one time or another. After a little break, I mount up, and hit the trail once again. It's time to shake it loose, and put this crazy experience behind me.

After a little while, I am easing back and getting into the ride again, when suddenly, I spook a flock of doves that were on the side of the road. Three of them just missed my windshield, and one flew right over my head and I could feel it hit my helmet. I hope it was okay. It sure scared the hell out of me, though.

One thing about these two lane roads is that you have to deal with those dangerous, enormous Beasts, that come barreling down the road at very fast speeds. I see them coming, so I grab hard on the handle bars and move as far away as I can to prepare for the huge blast of wind that almost knocks me off to the side of the road. Then, one second after the blast, I have to lean away from them, to avoid getting sucked under their gigantic tires. I knew of a friend who did not lean away fast enough, and the semi-truck just sucked him in. He did not make it, and I know he would not have wanted to live, with that kind of disaster.

With that behind me, I am back to enjoying the ride when all of a sudden my windshield turns yellow. "What in the heck," I am thinking. Then I see what happened. It's millions of butterflies, and they're all over me. I can hardly see through the windshield so I dismount and scrape some of them off. I have no windshield wipers, you know. Oh man, look at Pork! He is yellow all over now. I guess I am going to call him 'Old Yeller' heh-heh. I get back on the saddle again, and I am just now settling in and enjoying the whole experience, when all of a sudden, "bang-bang-bang." I get hit with what feels like 45 caliber bullets. It's not bullets, though, it's bugs. BIG bugs, at that! At these speeds, they hurt like hell. I guess they're huge because they have all this nice grazing land to eat. As I come around the corner, I see it: 'The 'Badlands' way off in the distance. "Oh man," I think . . . what a sight! (See Photos)

Badlands in the distance

What a sight

By this time it's damn hot outside. As I get closer to that barren land, it gets hotter and hotter. I think to myself that if I were on horseback when there were no roads to follow, I would get lost in that maze and just die out there. This is real barren land. Anyhow, I go right through the middle of it and enjoy the whole experience of being here. (See Photos)

Entrance to the Badlands

Extremely hot here

Awesome

Hot and isolated

I am now out of the Badlands and merging on to I-90. As I look out towards the horizon, I see black specks on the road as far as the eye can see. I can see that those specks are fellow bikers, by the thousands on the way to 'Mecca', home of the Harley, an annual pilgrimage to Sturgis. It's reported that over 550,000 bikers go there every year. Well, I am now on the freeway, so I kick in the spurs and get up to 90 mph again, when I start to notice that bikes are passing me up. What the hell I am doing 90 and those guys are passing me up . . . Damn!

Every once in awhile, I see some guy pulling his Harley on a trailer, and among Harley bikers this is a real no, no, that really pisses off some of the Harley bikers. I see them flipping the trailer guys off. We all know that you don't trailer a Harley. That is an insult to the bike . . . you ride the damn thing. I feel like flipping those guys off, too, but that's not my style. I have never flipped anyone off in my whole life. I wanted to many times, but I just can't get myself to do it. I would rather tell them off to their face than flip them off because it's so childish. Then I see what really burns me. Some idiot is wearing a Harley shirt, and here he is riding a (foreign bike). In my book, if you're going to wear the shirt, BUY THE DAMN BIKE!!! Anyhow, enough said.

Finally, I see the road sign "Rapid City," it's now 3:00 P.M., that was a five hour trip . . . a really short ride by my standards, I am so used to longer rides, I see my motel off to the side of the freeway. I yell at Pork, "WE MADE IT, WE'RE HERE!!!" as I squealed in to the motel parking lot. I jump off Pork, get my I.D. and walk up to the clerk and say, "Well, I made it!! I am so happy to be here, I finally made it." "What's your name?" she asked. "Joe Matus," I say. "Well, you're not due to arrive here until September," she says. "What?" I SCREAM, as my heart fell to the floor and this sickening feeling came over me. "Let me talk to the manager," I said. Finally the manager came out and said "Yep, we have you arriving in September." "September!" I scream out. "I rode my hog all the way here from California. Why in the world would I want to be here in September when the great Sturgis Rally is in August?"

"I made my reservations weeks in advance, and I explained over the phone why I was coming here." "I have the confirmation number right here, look." She looks, and then looks it up on her computer, and says, "Yep, you're scheduled for September, all right," she says, "And we have no rooms." "But I have a confirmation for $69.00 here." I scream, "Sixty-nine dollars, she screams back!!" "Our room rates in August are $300 a night, and that's the rate for all motels within a 300 mile radius of Sturgis." Then the light dawns, uh-oh, I am totally screwed now. I had better start putting on the old Joe Matus charm. So, I start sweet-talking and kissing butt. Here I am, down on my knees, begging, rolling on the ground, and crying like a baby. I'm saying, "But, but, but, me and Pork, we rode here all the way through wind and rain and mud, just to stay in your beautiful and wonderful establishment. PAALEESSSE, for the sake of poor Pork; just look at him. He is in miserable condition and he really needs to rest, because he is really a very sick Pig."

One look at Pork, and she relented. He always wins them over, heh-heh! She says, "I can only do it for $139 and I could get $300 dollars for the room." "OK," I say, as I hug and kiss her. Man, what an ordeal, as if I didn't have enough issues just getting here.

Anyhow, I unload Pork and go to the room. "WOW!!!" Pork really made an impression, because this is a wonderful room with a giant King size bed. Man, we struck gold here! I take a nice hot bath, and clean up. Boy it sure feels good to sit down and write about this experience while it is still daylight and I can remember all the events of the day. It's now about 6:00 P.M. so, I decided to ask the clerk to direct me to a nice restaurant. She referred me to one and off I go for my nice dinner and a good glass of wine. After dinner, I take a nice hot bath and settle down for the night in a very nice, huge and comfy bed. Before falling asleep, I set the clock for 5:30 A.M. This is the earliest yet. I want to get there early. I was told the traffic was a nightmare with thousands of people streaming into Sturgis.

Man, life is GREAT!!

Good Night,
Joe

Rapid City, South Dakota to Sturgis, South Dakota

Day Six … Sturgis

I decided to do some reading and found that: *Rapid City was founded (and originally known as "Hay Camp") in 1876 by a group of disappointed miners, who promoted their new city as the "Gateway to the Black Hills." John Breman and Samuel Scott, with a small group of men, laid out the site of the present Rapid City which was named for the spring-fed Rapid Creek that flows through it. A square mile was measured off and the six blocks in the center were designated as a business section. Committees were appointed to bring in prospective merchants and their families to locate in the new settlement. The city soon began selling supplies to miners and pioneers. Its location on the edge of the Plains and Hills and its large river valley made it the natural hub of railroads arriving in the late 1880s from both the south and east. By 1900, Rapid City had survived a boom and bust and was establishing itself as an important regional trade center for the upper Midwest.*

The alarm sounded on time so I forced myself out of bed. As my feet hit the floor, I realized that I had been a real bad boy. My usual regimen at home is to get up every morning, take a nice hot shower, and do my regular stretches. I suffer from a really bad back, and if I don't do the stretches, my back will give out on me and lay me up for days. I have been in such a hurry to get here that I have neglected to do my stretches, and now my back is saying, "You screwed up, boy!" DAMN!!! I hurt, and I have this horrible feeling that if I lay down again, I will not be able to leave this room.

So I walk very gingerly to the tub, and soak for a while. Then I do my usual stretches . . . very very carefully because I do not want to throw my back out now. So, I get dressed and wrap myself with a back brace, which I always carry with me in case of a back problem. I go outside and get on Pork. Now he is giving me a hard time, but finally starts. So off we go to the gas station for his chow. He pigs out, and as we start to leave the gas station he sputters, he chokes, he spits and he quits. "DAMN IT PORK!!! GET ME TO STURGIS, PAALEESEE, AND THEN I WILL TAKE YOU TO THE HOSPITAL, I PROMISE!!" I SCREAM!! He relents and starts, and off we go, but not without sputtering some more. Damn Pig, he is never happy. He is letting me know who the boss is. We get there and the place is enormous, so I walk around and check out the town. Pork is right next to the telephone pole on the left. Diamond shape carburetor filter. (See Photos)

It's 8 A.M. at Sturgis

The city of Sturgis was founded in 1878 as a boom town catering to off-duty soldiers just outside the U.S. Cavalry's Fort Meade and is named for Ft. Meade's commander, Colonel Samuel D. Sturgis. Later it became a port of entry to the Black Hills goldfields. Today, Sturgis is known worldwide as "Motorcycle City USA."

I love the statue

Quite a lineup

Me and Pork down town Sturgis

Keeping the world on two wheels

It's getting busy

I like making new friends

There goes my buddy

Can you see the dog in the window?

Bikes as far as you can see

Beautiful statue

Nicely done

I saw a Harley Davidson building and went in to ask if they do repairs. He said, "they don't do repairs and the dealership is miles away, and they are booked ahead for days." I asked if there is anyone here who can work on my Harley. He said, "there are a couple of guys down the street who work on Harley's and they are set up in a tent." I thanked him and went looking for the place. I found it and talked to the man in charge. I told him my problems with Pork. I asked him to give Pork some new blood (Oil) and a new heart (Spark Plugs). I told him that Pork has a sore throat (Filter), and that he squeals a lot (New Brake Pads). "Good," the man says. "Bring him in and we'll take care of him." So I go get the pig and tell him, "Seeeeee, I'm keeping my promise." (See Photo)

Pork in the hospital

What the man in charge did not tell me was that there was a waiting list, and I was third in line, so I would have to wait for a few hours. OK, so I leave Pork, and walk around to kill time. As I am walking around I notice a bike wash area. I am thinking, "Hmmmm, Pork is pretty dirty, but after all he is a pig!!" I said to myself, "Come on now, he needs to be cleaned up." So a few hours later, when all his work is done and I go to pick him up, I pay the price (which was not cheap) and I take him to get a real bath, which I know he will hate! He does not like to get wet!! TOO BAD!!

I see that nothing is cheap in Sturgis, not even the bath, 'Duhhhh.' As I am waiting for him to get cleaned up, I notice that right next door is a paint shop. Well, I have always wanted to remove the old icon and replace it with a new icon of New York and the Golden Gate Bridge. The two of us took a trip to New York and back, a few years ago. "Hmmmm, I think . . . I will have it done!" I spoke to the painter and told him what I had in mind, he says, "sure I can do that." (Sure, for a hefty price I bet, I say to myself.) "Oh well. Do it." Then I said, "How long will it take?" "About five hours," he says. "You have to let the paint dry before you can ride him." Pork is now cleaned up. (See Photo)

After his bath

So, I roll him over to the paint shop and leave him there. Of course the painter did not tell me that he had other jobs already waiting. By the time he got to Pork, a few hours had already passed. Now that he is getting to Pork, it will be another five hours. Damn! I only wanted to spend a few hours here, and then check out the other sights here in South Dakota. I got to Sturgis at 7:00 A.M. and did not leave until 7:30 P.M. I was hanging around for twelve and a half hours. Now I have blisters on my feet and I know Sturgis like the back of my hand. (Go ahead ask me anything.) The artist did a pretty good job. (See Photos)

Old Icon   **New Icon**

Well I paid the man, mounted up, and off we go. We are now on the highway heading east when I noticed that way off in the distance I can see a small red glow. "Hmmmm! I wonder what that small red glow is." As I get closer and closer, the amber glow gets bigger and bigger. Now I see it! It is a semi-truck, the whole cabin and trailer is in engulfed in flames. Man, its right in the middle of the freeway and everyone has given it a lot of space, it has backed up the westbound traffic for miles and miles. It's now dark, and I can see head lights for what seems like a hundred miles, what an awesome sight. Thank God I am going east, and the traffic is not a factor for me. Pork enjoyed his stay in the hospital, and is now running like a top. Hallelujah! Finally the pig is happy, and so am I.

Yours always,
Joe

P.S. "Hmmmm," I wonder, "Are they going to let me stay another night?" Remember, I was only scheduled for two nights, and everything in this town is booked up.

Rapid City, South Dakota to points of interest

Day Seven … The Black Hills

Another sleepless night! I tossed and turned all night, because I was worried that I was going to be evicted, and I was only scheduled for two nights. Because of Pork, I did not get to see any of the sights outside of town, and spent all day just waiting for them to finish working on him. I do not want to leave just yet, and this morning I woke up really tired and concerned.

What to do? Well first things first. Get that important cup of coffee and wake up and then go talk to the manager. After I enjoyed my coffee, I decided now is the time. I went up to the clerk and said, "I would like to talk to the manager." She said "OK" and disappeared. Out comes this lady and she says "Can I help you?" I said, "Yes, I would like to talk to the manager." She says "I am the manager." "Well, you're not the lady I talked to before." She says "No, I am the other manager." "Oh, my God," I say to myself. I had just won over the other manager and now here is a complete stranger (I am not ready for this!). Suddenly I have to turn on the old Joe Matus charm again, but I did not have time to prepare for this. I couldn't use the old 'look at poor Pork he is miserable line,' because he is looking really good right about now with his new paint job and recent bath.

Suddenly I throw myself on the floor, and stick my bare feet into the air and cry out!! "Look at my poor feet. They have blisters on them because that miserable pig was sick, and I had to walk all around Sturgis while he was being worked on and I had to walk for hours waiting on him. I have not had a chance to look around your beautiful town," "WOE-IS-ME!" I cry out! "Oh, you poor thing", she says, as she throws a few Band-Aids at me and says, "Here, put these on those blisters.

I will give you one more night, but it's going to cost you more money," she says. "Hallelujah," I cry out. In the meantime I am saying to myself "#&%*^%$ screwed again." Oh well, at least I have a bed for the night. I am feeling a lot better now. So, I go in and take a shower and hit the road. It's about 10:00 A.M., but first things first. I must find a shoe repair shop because I had worn out the back heels of my boots with all the walking I did yesterday. I was not kidding, I did have blisters. Anyhow, I found a shoe repair shop and had my boots fixed. I mounted up and off I went to see Mt. Rushmore. So, into the Black Hills I ride. I could not have asked for a more beautiful day. The sky was clear, the air was warm, and it was so perfect that I even wore a short sleeve shirt. I am having a wonderful ride right now. Man, this is it! I arrived at Mt. Rushmore and checked out the sights. (See Photos)

Mt. Rushmore

I finally got here

Then I decided to go see Crazy Horse. After a short but marvelous ride through the Black Hills, I arrived at the gates. The lady said "You are so lucky, they are about to blast in about 5 minutes, and if you hurry, you can catch it. They only do this once a week and your timing is perfect!" So I gun it, race to the parking lot, jump off Pork, grab the camera and make the shot just as they blasted. A bit later, I checked out the museum and saw a short movie about how it all came to be. (See Photos)

Crazy horse

Just before the blast

What it will look like after completion

Crazy Horse in the distance

Crazy Horse motorcycle

Deadwood

I know her

I decided to go and check out Deadwood, where Wild Bill Hickok met his demise: *Deadwood was founded in 1876 during the gold rush boom. The city attracted miners and the lawless likes of Calamity Jane and Wild Bill Hickok. But after the initial reckless phase of the gold rush, the city settled down to enjoy its newly accumulated wealth. The town is small because hilly geographic constricted expansion, and the wealthy built up the downtown area of Main Street. In September of 1878 a devastating fire destroyed most of the wooden structures of the downtown. In the quarter century after the great fire, Deadwood experienced an extraordinary building boom.*

While riding Pork through the Black Hills, I experienced what I would have to say, was one of the most beautiful and most inspiring rides I have had. I rode for hours through the middle of the Black Hills. The road was pure cement, and as smooth as glass. I could not even feel one little bump on the road. The air was fresh and the smell of the trees was all around me. Those trees were as green, as green can get. All the trees were of the same kind, and they were so, so green, that when a cloud went over head, the trees in the valley became black. I guess that is why they call it the Black Hills.

In the hours that I rode through the mountains, not one bug ever hit the windshield. The whole thing was magical, so serene and so peaceful, and I really felt that I was one with God. There were hours of soft, winding curves, that made this ride perfect for motorcycles. I felt so bad for the people who were trapped in their cages (cars) as they went by. I almost felt like screaming at them, "get out of your car, get on a bike, feel the wind in your face and smell the wonder of this enchanting place." It was a very moving experience, and it could easily bring a tear to your eyes, I know it did that to me.

No wonder the Lakota consider this place to be a very sacred place. If you're a biker, you have not lived until you have ridden through the Black Hills of South Dakota. I thank God for this experience, and I have made a huge deposit into my bank. (My memory bank that is). (See Photos)

My Pal Smokey

Gorgeous lake

Please do yourself a favor while you still can and are able. Store as much fun and experience into your memory banks as you can. For one day, when you're old and not able to do much, and you're stuck in an old people's home, you can sit back in your rocking chair, make a withdrawal, and relive some of your wonderful experiences.

I can just see me in an old people's home. Sitting in a rocking chair, and smiling like crazy! People will go by and say, "What the hell is he smiling about?" Well folks, I will be making a withdrawal, and reliving my ride through the magical and marvelous valleys of the Black Hills. As I leave Deadwood, and merge on to I-90 (See Map) I am now back to reality. Once again I encounter the thousands and thousands of other bikers, who have made their way here to Mecca, home of the Harley experience. I am thinking, it's only Thursday, and they are already here. "Damn . . . don't these people have jobs?" My God people, it's not even the weekend yet.

Well, I made a decision right there and then, I have to get out of Dodge before all the weekend warriors show up, and this place becomes unbearable. Some of these rich cats even have their bikes flown in, so they do not have to make the long ride. What a bunch of sissies!!

By the time I get to my room its 4:15 P.M. It's been a glorious 6 hour day, and Pork and I are in hog heaven. "Hmmmm, I wonder what I am going to do tomorrow." I have no plans whatsoever. I have no schedule to keep, no place to run to, and no appointment or reservation to keep. I am not pressed for time to get up and hurry. Ahhh, life is good.

Maybe in the morning I will just get up, look out the window and decide then. Who knows? Or maybe I will just go whichever way the wind blows. Hey, wait! Someone told me once that Montana is beautiful this time of year. "Hmmmm," that sounds interesting. Watch out Montana, here cometh the Lone Rider and his wild white stallion, Silver and sidekick, PorkChop.

HI-O-SILVER and good night to you all! Thank you Lord for making this a wonderful, special day for me. Bless all my friends and loved ones. I am telling you . . . that ride was very spiritual.

Yours Always,
Joe

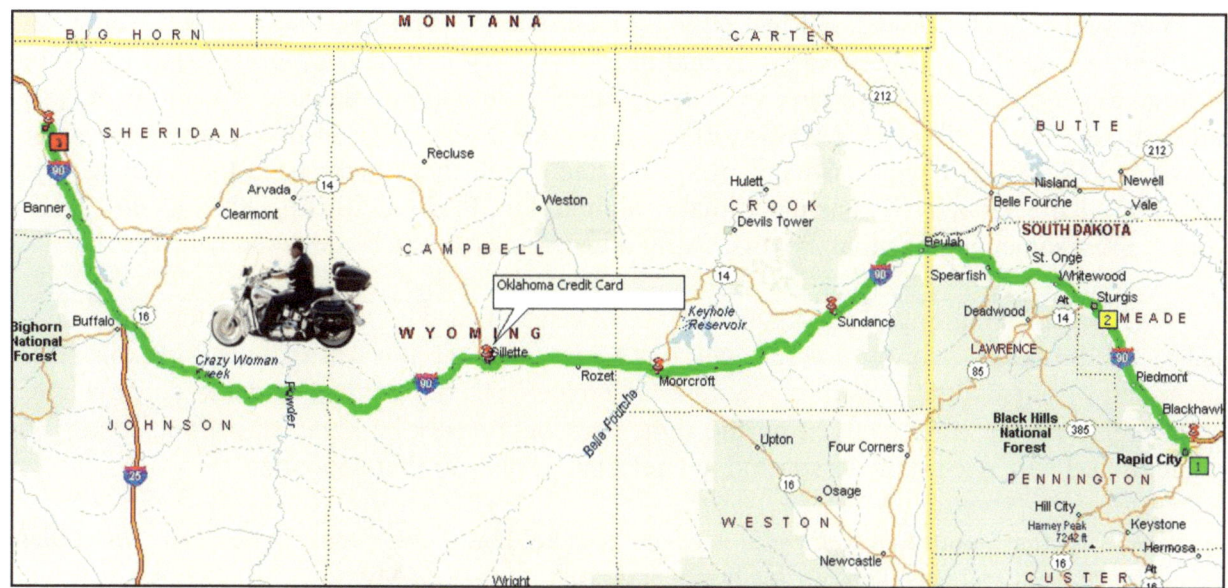

Rapid City, South Dakota to Sheridan, Wyoming

Day Eight: Diamonds On PorkChop

Well I got up sore and tired from my wonderful day of adventure yesterday. I lagged around till about 10:00 A.M. before I checked out of the motel. I really hated to leave Sturgis and the whole surrounding area. It's a wonderful place to visit and ride bikes, needless to say there were thousands of bikes here. Everyone was having a good time and I talked to people that came from all over the world and as far away as Spain and Germany.

I loaded Pork and bid everyone farewell and thanked them for their hospitality. I was sad to leave, and as I put more and more distance between me, and Sturgis I saw fewer and fewer bikes. The weather was beautiful and everything was fine with my world. As I grabbed a handful of throttle and hit 50 mph, PorkChop made his transformation and became the wild white stallion named Silver. Now, I am on my Iron Horse and off we went; 60, then 75, now 80 and now where he likes it best, 90 miles per hour. As we entered the State of Wyoming I was in the zone, that blissful place of pure concentration and focus in and on the present. No lingering nostalgia, not anticipating the future, just sailing over the plains of Wyoming. (See Map)

As I was speeding along on that endless black asphalt, I knew full well that I was breaking every damn speeding rule in the books. I saw so many bikers being pulled over by cops. The cops were out like vultures just waiting to pounce on bikers. The poor guys, I really felt bad for them because the cops were giving them tickets. As Silver and I went flying by at 90 miles an hour I heard one of the bikers screaming, "Why don't you go after that guy? Look at the sucker go, he must be doing 90 mph." I saw the cop look in my direction, and I was sure he was going to stop what he was doing, jump in his patrol car, and come after me or at least call ahead to his buddies and yell, "stop that guy on the white iron horse." It was a constant watch looking out for Smokey and it took a little bliss off my ride. Oh well, what the hell, as I grabbed a hand full of throttle.

You know, in all fairness, if I had gotten pulled over by the cops, I sure as hell would have deserved the ticket. I had been speeding and breaking every law on the highway and I was long overdue to get one. I would not have even complained about getting the ticket. Well, maybe just a little. Like . . . "PAAALEASSSSEEEE . . . DON'T GIVE ME A TICKET . . . PAAAALEESSSEEE I will wash and wax your tractor (all these hicks have them out here you know) and I'll even babysit your illegitimate children, but, PAAALASEEE DON'T GIVE ME A TICKET" or something like that, not that I would beg, or anything like that, heh-heh.

As I was planning my plea bargain speech, I noticed that the wind was starting to become a real factor. It became stronger and stronger. The worst thing about it was that the wind was hitting Silver and I from all directions. It was a miserable experience not knowing what to do. If you lean to the right and the wind hits you on the right you could easily be knocked off your bike. You would think I would learn my lesson and not get such a late start, but nooooooo!

It was all that I could do to try and stay on the bike. It was the strongest buffeting wind that I have experienced and this went on for hours and hours non-stop. My arms, shoulders, neck, wrist and my hands were aching so bad from the constant struggle trying to stay centered on the bike. Even worse than the wind were the beasts (semi-trucks) that prowl the freeway just waiting to suck you under their tires. As you go by these beasts, there is a small tornado type effect called vortices that want to spin you around like a top that could easily throw you off your bike. For example; when driving your car and a semi-truck passes by, you feel your car move a little. Now imagine what it does to you when you are on a bike. "So, why do you pass them, you ask?" Because the damn things are in my way, darn it!! If I stay behind them, I will never get to my destination. This was a continual issue and it was excruciating and exhausting. However, these challenges are the parts that I reflect on the most when I am home safe and sound, this is what makes the journey so memorable.

I have noticed that in some states the helmet laws are different and you do not have to wear them. Consequently, 98% of the bikers that I have run into on this trip are not wearing helmets. I think it is a good idea to always wear one. However I have been known not to wear one from time to time and you might consider me stupid for not wearing one and for going 90 miles per hour, but I can't help it. I have a need for speed and when you are a pilot like me, you are used to going fast. I know it's stupid and I agree with you (this time only).

After a while, I hear the Pork start to whine about his chow. So, I pull into this gas station just out of Sundance, and noticed this sign. (See Photo)

The sign says it all

Sorry about the lack of pictures but that's all there was, prairie, prairie and more prairie. The sign said that Devils Tower was two and a half hours out of my way, so I decided not to go there this time, but what the hey! Oh, guess what? In the convenience store, next to the gas station where I had stopped to get gas, I finally found what I had been looking for the whole time I have been on this journey. "Hallelujah." "Praise the Lord!" I found me an Oklahoma Credit Card!! A.K.A., a rubber hose used to siphon gas out of peoples cars, tee-hee. I have scored! I feel a lot better now, since I only have a 5 gallon tank and gas stations are so few and far between in these here parts. Now as I am riding along, fighting to stay on the bike, I noticed that way off in the distance, (See Photo) some of the clouds that I thought were so pretty, are now starting to get really nasty looking. I look way off into the horizon and see a little glint of light. "Oh!" I say, "it's just a car's headlights going off and on." I figured that the car was just going up and down on those rolling hills because the light would appear and then disappear. As I got closer and closer I realize that, "HEY!!! Wait, that's not headlights, that's LIGHTNING!! . . . DAMN!!! Not again, PLEASE, not again!" I say to myself as I am barreling down the freeway at 90 miles an hour, heading right into the mouth of the storm. (See Photo)

The storm is coming

Pretty soon, there is this little spot of water on my windshield then another, then another. Then, all of a sudden, there is a bolt of lightning, and down it comes in buckets. "DAMN! Doesn't it ever just rain in these parts?" "Must it always come down in buckets?" Within minutes, I am totally drenched, from head to toe. Now there is lightning going off here and there and all around me with no place to hide. It's becoming a real concern for me, as Silver is all white and chrome. Well, actually, he's all chrome, and I understand that lightning likes shiny things. I am thinking, "Oh man, we are the only ones on this plain and we are shining like a neon light. I get this feeling that they are going to find me and Silver all crispy and well done lying on the side of the road, sizzled by a bolt of lightning!"

I am thinking that in California I can cut across the state in a few hours. However, the states I have been going through take a day or more to cross. Damn, there is no place to hide from this storm as far as I can see, which is not far with this downpour. WAIT!! I just went by a sign and it said Sheridan 22 miles . . . 22 MILES!!? Another 20 minutes of this pouring rain NOOOOOOO!! I can't take anymore I already have webbed feet. Oh well, I have no choice so I give Silver the spurs, and off we go into the storm even faster. Finally, I see the turnoff and I take it and pull into the first motel I see which is a Motel 6. I jumped off Pork and ran inside out of the rain. I was totally sopping wet standing there shivering and inquiring about the cost of the room. "$92 DOLLARS," I SCREAM!!! This is Motel 6, and we are in Wyoming next to the Montana border, far away from Sturgis. What's with this outrageous price?" "I know where we are," he says politely. "Check out the other hotels. They are a lot more expensive than us." "Yeah, like I was going to go out in that rain again," I thought to myself. I wouldn't even go out in it if I was in a car. Oh well, screwed again, story of my life. Anyhow, I unloaded Pork while it was pouring. Have you ever unloaded your car while it was pouring cats and dogs? You know, like you run in and run out of the rain. It's not fun, but I didn't care. I was soaked anyway.

Into the storm we ride

Finally after unloading Pork and piling all my gear in the lobby, I grabbed the elevator to get to my room, and there was a lady in the elevator with me as we headed up a couple of floors. I could see that she was giving me plenty of space. I realized again that I must stink to high heavens, what with all of my wet leathers. I finally found my room and proceeded to rip off my leathers and again found it extremely difficult; wet leather just wants to stick to you. I finally got everything off of me and took a very hot shower. I sure as heck did not want to get a cold, certainly not now.

When I got out of the shower, I found information about this place and found that: *Sheridan was named by founder J. D. Loucks for his Civil War commander, General Sheridan. And was established in 1882 and was born during the cattle boom, a town brought to life by aristocratic cattle barons. The Bradford Brinton Memorial Museum in the nearby hamlet of Big Horn and is a classic example of their lifestyle.*

This neo-colonial house built by the aristocratic Scottish brothers William and Malcolm Moncreiffe, was headquarters for their Quarter Circle A Ranch. The Moncreiffes played polo on what was probably the first polo field in the nation at the nearby ranch home of their English kin, the Wallops. Bradford Brinton, a wealthy gentleman from Chicago, bought the Moncreiffe ranch in the 1920's, enlarged it and filled it to overflowing with a spectacular collection of Western art. Although it may not feel like it belongs here, the museum is an authentic piece of Wyoming history and an interesting place to visit.

Within Sheridan are other pieces of this upper class heritage, including the Kendrick mansion preserved as the Trail End Historic Center, and the wonderful architecture of the historic Sheridan Inn, whose prominent guests included Presidents Roosevelt, Taft, and Hoover.

After relaxing a bit I looked out the window and lo and behold, it had stopped raining. Well, of course story of my life. But WAIT!! "What's that?" There are diamonds all over PorkChop. "OH MY GOD!!" He is loaded with diamonds, and he looks beautiful with all the jewelry wrapped all around him. So I grab my camera and head out to take a picture of him and his beautiful diamonds. As I passed the desk clerk's counter, I noticed a huge puddle of water on this side of the counter, where I had been standing. I told the clerk about the water and went outside to take a picture of Pork's new jewelry. If you blow up the picture, you can really see the diamonds. The sun was hitting him, and the raindrops looked like diamonds. (See Photo) As soon as I took the pictures, it started pouring again so I went back inside and noticed that the clerk had a mop and was cleaning up the wet spots that I had left all the way to the elevator. I asked him, "Where is your finest restaurant?" He made a suggestion, and then I asked him to please call me a cab.

Diamonds on Pork

I ride hard and I ride long hours. I have made it a point to always treat myself to a nice dinner with a fine glass of wine, and I deserve it.

After the long ordeal with the nasty weather, it is one thing getting caught in the rain, but I'll be damned if I will go out in it on purpose when it's raining. I checked into the motel at around 4:15 P.M. which made today's ride a 6 hour ride . . . a short ride by my standards. But what the hell, it was pouring out and I was really miserable and cold. I am smart enough to come in out of the rain. When the cab finally showed up it was still raining heavily. I jumped in the cab and told him, "Take me to your finest restaurant." He says, "What are you in the mood for?" I said, "A good steak and a fine glass of wine." Then he says, "Have you ever tried buffalo?" I said "Nope!" "Well then, I will take you to a place that has a good buffalo steak." When we arrived at the restaurant, I jumped out and ran in, because it was still raining like mad! I went inside, and the place was packed. The waitress tells me that it's going to be a 20 minute wait, Damn, I think, what can I do? I have no wheels, and its pouring out. I had no choice, so I sat and waited. I finally got a table that sat four people, which made me feel bad for taking up so much space.

I settled in, ordered a Buffalo steak and a nice Cabernet, (by the way the steak was lean and delicious). All of a sudden I noticed that my fingertips were really hurting. I looked down at my fingers, to see that the tips were all sunburned from the knuckles to the tips. It was so hot during the initial start of my ride, that I put on these gloves that have the finger tips cut off because they were cooler, but who would have thought to put suntan lotion on their fingertips? Darn it, it hurts. Suddenly the waitress came over and asked me if I wouldn't mind sharing the table, I said, "not at all." I felt good about sharing the table and maybe meeting some new, interesting folks.

I met a husband and wife from Canada, a real nice couple and they asked all the usual questions. Where I was from, etc. I told them I was from California and that I had gone to Sturgis and was on my way home. The man got all excited and said that was awesome and that he also owned a motorcycle it was a (foreign bike).

He went on about how impressed he was that I had ridden so far to attend the rally and how he had always wanted to do something like that. When I told him about my bike trip to New York, that I took all by myself, he just about fell off his chair. He went on and on, about how he admired my fortitude. He told me how he wished he could do that. I thought to myself, you could if you would just get off your big fat butt instead of just riding on the weekends. I ended up telling them how nice it was to meet them, and I left the restaurant. I called the cab and of course it was pouring really hard when he showed up.

Have you ever looked out your window and it was raining so hard that you could not see across the street? Well that's how it was. The cab showed up and I made a run for the van. I grabbed the door handle and yanked and yanked on it. It wouldn't open and man that rain was coming down in buckets! I finally realized that I was dealing with one of those stupid doors that slide open. Damn thing! Now I am really soaked.

—◆—

As we get to the motel I look over at Pork and he is being inundated with torrents of rain, poor guy. I yell at him "Don't worry Pork, I will take good care of you tomorrow and give you some good chow." (gas) Cowboys in the old days considered their horse their best friend. They would spend many months out on the western plains with only each other for company and they would talk to their horse. You probably talk to your dogs, cats and other pets at home. It's easy to develop a bond with them and so we talk to them. Besides, who would be taking a trip like this by themselves unless they were nuts . . . like me!

Pork and I spend many, many hours on the saddle and I have no one to talk to, so Pork is my constant companion. He takes care of me and I take care of him. . . . So there, that confirms that I am totally crazy, but I don't care, I knew that long ago. I beat you to it.

So now that we have that all cleared up, let me continue. I hit the sack about 12:30 and laid there and turned and twisted and turned and twisted and could not go to sleep. I did not sleep a wink all night. HONEST! I laid there and thought about everything under the sun.

As a parent, I thought about my children and how they are doing. I worry about them and I love them dearly. They have been good kids, never giving me any problems. I am so blessed to have them. You never really quit being a parent, even though my children are all grown, and have families of their own. I still think of them as my babies and I still worry about their well-being. I thought about my life. I have had my ups and downs but who hasn't? I am healthy and not under any medication whatsoever. Over all, I have been blessed and if I should not make it back, becoming road kill along the highway, I know that I have put my affairs in order and my kids will be well taken care of.

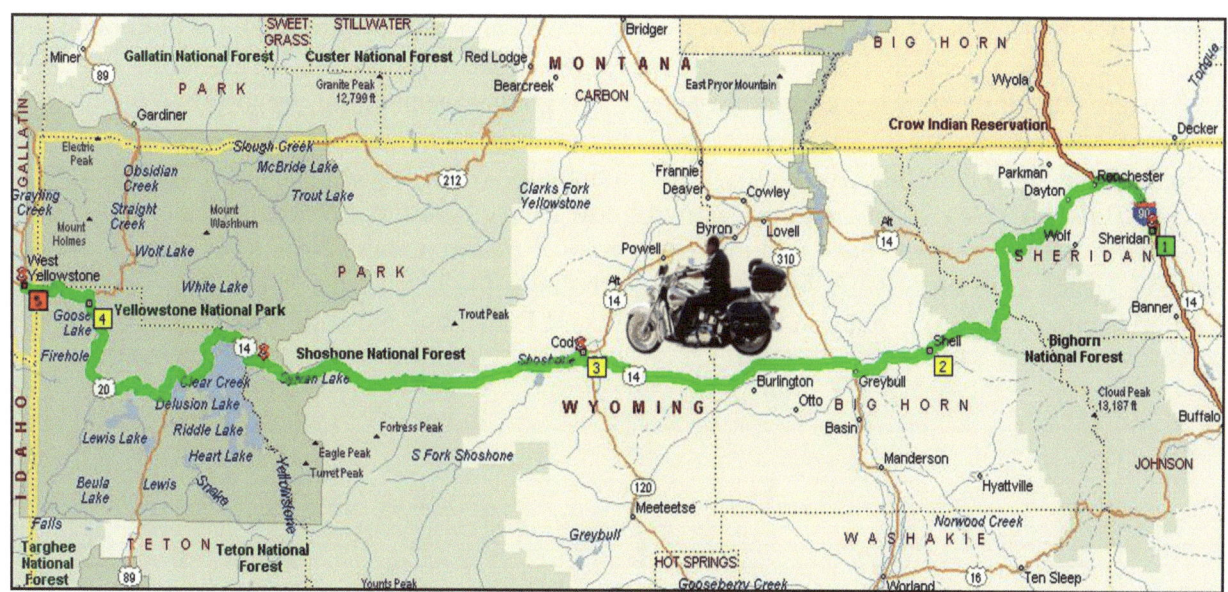

Sheridan, Wyoming to W. Yellowstone, Montana

Day Nine … Yellowstone

I looked over at the clock and damn it!! It's 4:30 A.M. and I have not slept one wink. I guess I might as well get up. I looked outside, and its dark, so I take a shower, get my stuff and load up Pork. By this time its 7:00 A.M. and it looks real nasty outside with heavy, dark, low clouds as far as you can see. "Darn it!" I go down to talk to the desk clerk, and tell him that I'm thinking of taking a short cut. I plan on going over the Big Horn Mountains. (See Map) "Oh heavens! I would not do that!" he says. "That mountain is over 13,000 feet, and it stormed yesterday." "Duhhhh, I was in it," I was thinking to myself. "It snowed really hard on that mountain, and some guy hit black ice and went over the edge to his death yesterday," he said. He went on to say, "I have a four wheel Jeep and I would not go over that mountain. If I were you, I would go the long way around." I thanked him, mounted Pork, and took him down the road for his chow.

Well, that damn Porker started sputtering, spitting, and choking all over again. "Damn it Pork," I screamed. "I just spent a fortune on you. What the hell is going on?" I decided he's probably got an ulcer (a hair line crack on a valve) and I am going to have to take him to a specialist when I get him home. He still does this every time I feed him. As Silver, he has no problems once we are tearing across the plains. Only as Pork, does he have a problem at startups!

We hit the road anyway, I grab a hand full of throttle and Silver comes to life! As we speed along at 90, I start to look for Smokey and all of a sudden, I start to sing. . . . *"Get your motor running. Head out on the highway looking' for adventure, and whatever comes our way." "Born to be wild. . . . Born to be wild. . . . " Come on, sing along with me. . . . "Get your motor running. Head out on the highway looking for adventure and whatever comes our way." "Born to be wild … Born to be wild. . . . "

That's cool, huh? When I went to New York a few years ago (just Pork and I), I would break out singing. . . . *"Me and Pork all the way cross the USA . . . Me and Pork all the way cross the USA. . . . " I sang that all the way home, as well. "Hey! You gotta do something, or you'll go nuts!"

So, I settled in for the long way around the mountain, when I hear this inner voice say "GO WEST, YOUNG MAN!" "GO WEST!" Now I know I have heard that somewhere before. "Damn that clerk!" He never should have told me not to go over that mountain. Now I am going to do just that. So, I yank hard on Silver's left rein, and he bolts to the left, as we ride off into the sunset. Well, it's actually morning, but you know what I mean! Down into the valley we ride. (See Photo)

Mountains looming ahead

As we ride into the valley, I noticed that we are on a gentle downward slope and I have this foreboding feeling that the mountain is beckoning us to come closer and closer as it slowly draws us into its bowels. As we approach the base of the mountain I give Silver the spurs and we start our ascent. As we approach 1,000 feet, my face starts to hurt because of the frigid cold air. I have no choice but to stop and pull over and put on a face mask for protection against the cold. Now we are at 6,000 feet, 7,000 feet, and it is so cold that I can't feel my hand on the throttle. It is so painfully cold and now we are at 8,000 feet. I jump off Pork and rip off my gloves and put my hands right on top of the engine to warm them up. I put them within an inch of the exhaust pipes, just to get some feeling back in them. Under normal conditions, you cannot even get your hands near the engine or the pipes without burning yourself, and here I am with my hands an inch away and I could hardly feel the heat. I kept the engine running and gave it full throttle, just to generate more heat, but it didn't seem to help.

Now that we are over 9,000 feet, and we come around a bend, I scream out "WHAT THE HELL!!!" You won't believe this, but, HONEST TO GOD!!! they are doing road construction up here. They stop me and say "You have to wait here for 20 minutes" YOU HAVE GOT TO BE KIDDING!!! DAMN IT ANYHOW! So, I get off Pork, put my hands back on his tail (the exhaust pipe), and try to keep my hands warm, all the while jumping around like a grasshopper, trying to stay warm. I was burning gas, but I dare not turn Pork off, for fear he would choke and not want to start (because of ice in the carburetor). He was already giving me problems earlier, and that would be all I needed to have him quit on me up here.

That's all I need for them Valley Folk to say, "Yep, they found this frozen pig and this frozen Mexican up there in that thar mountain."

Finally, they allowed Pork and I to proceed. As Pork and I descended into the valley, it got warmer and warmer, and I started to take off clothes. Hey, not all of them, just my jacket and gloves and such.

I kick in the spurs and Silver springs to action as we race across the valley and into the land of Cody, Wyoming, land of Buffalo Bill Cody. (See Photo)

Buffalo Bill stayed in the hotel behind me

Pork and I once rode solo to Colorado to see the Buffalo Bill Museum and grave site where he and his wife are buried, I have always been interested in him. I pulled into the first gas station I saw, as I was running low after wasting fuel on top of the mountain. I had my apple and a swig of water and fed the Porker. Damn if he didn't start his usual sputtering right after I fed him. I am really getting tired of this. I saw a Harley Dealership and decided to ask for a mechanic. They did not have one but they had plenty of tee shirts. So, what could I do? I bought one!

I mounted up and pointed Silver into the heart of Yellowstone and away we went. "HI-O-SILVER. . . . AWAYYYYYYY." The only thing I can say about Yellowstone is that, if you have never been there, it has got to be one of the things on your bucket list. A very dear friend gave me a book for my birthday. The title was: "1000 Things You Should Do Before You Die." The first thing on the list was 'visit Yellowstone.' It is one of God's masterpieces and you owe it to yourself to see it. It will bring a tear to your eye.

In fact, I was so impressed that I stopped at a gift shop and bought a mount to snap onto my bike so I could video the whole experience. It ended up not working so well, the movie turned out all shaky. If you plan to go through Yellowstone be sure to give yourself 3 to 4 hours, because those damn tourists stop and photograph every stone, tree, lizard and squirrel they see. Of course, this backs up traffic for miles. You would think these people never saw a damn squirrel before.

Yellowstone

Into Yellowstone we ride

Seconds away

Look for the rainbow

In the mist

Grazing Buffalo

The Corp of Discovery led by Lewis and Clark were the first whites to explore the greater Yellowstone region. Among them was one of the most celebrated hunters and woodsmen of that period, John Colter. On the return of the expedition in 1908, Colter returned to the Yellowstone and trapped this region and in doing so became the first white visitor to see what is now Yellowstone National Park. Upon his return, his "tales" were so unbelievable that no author or mapmaker would publish it for fear of scrutiny amongst their peers. Colters' stories about the wonders and wildlife, led the fur traders to explore the Yellowstone regions. Most of the mountain men during that era were experienced in trapping and survival, they were also illiterate. Fortunately, Osborn Russell was unique, he knew how to trap, read and write and his journals are the earliest accounts of the Yellowstone region.

"There is something in the wild scenery of this valley which I cannot describe: but the impressions made upon my mind while gazing from a high eminence on the surrounding landscape one evening as the sun was gently gliding behind the western mountain and casting its gigantic shadows across the vale were such as time can never efface. For my own part I almost wished I could spend the remainder of my days in a place like this where happiness and contentment seemed to reign in wild romantic splendor" - Lamar Valley, Osborne Russell 1835.

Finally, we get through Yellowstone, after a grueling 3 to 4 hour trip of stop and go. It was beautiful however, and well worth it! I would do it again in a heartbeat. Now we are entering Montana. (See Photo)

Montana and miles of gravel road

We are now heading into the town of Gallatin. I see a Day's Inn, so I dismount and walk inside to ask for a room. "$218 BUCKS I SCREAMED." "WHYYYYYYY?" "This is not Sturgis and this is not the Hilton. This is a Day's Inn for Christ sakes." "Nope," he says, "But look out the window, that is Yellowstone."

"Damn! Just a minute," I say. So I go out to talk to Pork. "WHAT?" he squeals, "Are you crazy or nuts or both? We have been on the road nonstop for 12 hours. (It is now 7:45 P.M.) You're crazy if you think we are going to run around town, looking for another room." "If you don't take this room, I just won't start tomorrow!!" Damn Pig! How in the hell do you fight logic like that? So, I went back in and said, "I will take the room." The man says, "You're lucky, because that's the last room we have." "Sure," I think to myself. "That's what they all say, just to make you feel good about spending that kind of money." Oh well, screwed again.

The room was nice and clean. I unloaded Pork, took a nice hot shower, and then asked the desk clerk, "Where is your finest restaurant?" He says, "Just three blocks down this street." I thanked him and I started walking towards it. Well, hell he didn't tell me that each block was two miles long. By the time I got there I was exhausted.

RAINBOW TROUT!! I had not had that in years. I had a nice glass of Chardonnay, and the trout was the best I had in many a year. "Ahhh, life is GRAND!" I didn't even miss my steak dinner. Walking back, I reflected on the 12 hour, non-stop ride to get here.

It was a real grueling ride over that mountain, but they don't call me "Iron Butt Matus" for nothing ... heh-heh. I turned in for the night, and was sound asleep, when, all of a sudden, I hear Pork squealing his lungs out (his alarm went off). I thought I was dreaming, but no! It was him. I looked at the clock, and it was 1:30 A.M. I jumped out of bed and rushed to the window, but I did not see anyone. Everything looked normal so I went back to bed. Then, around 3:00 A.M. he started squealing again so I jumped out of bed again and rushed to the window, still I did not see anyone. I always make it a point to bed Pork down right next to my window, so I can keep an eye on him.

As you can well imagine, I did not sleep a wink the whole night, worrying whether Pork would start squealing his lungs out again. You have never heard a squeal like Pork's. He can wake up the dead for two miles in every direction. I was afraid that the Motel Management would come banging on the door to evict me and Pork, right out on his pig's ear for waking up all of the tenants.

While I lay there, I was contemplating what was the most arduous part of my whole journey and I guess I would have to say that going through all those horrible miles of muddy slime, knee deep in yuck, had to be the worst. And I was wondering why it was so hard for me to get through that, and then all of a sudden it hit me, That DAMN PIG! Of course! I bet if you asked him, he would say that was the best part of the trip for him. He was in Hog Heaven, wallowing through miles of disgustingly muddy, yucky slime. Damn Pig! No wonder he squealed like a pig when we finally got out of it. All this time, I thought he was squealing about the mud in his fenders. He just did not want to leave. He was in Hog Heaven and he just wanted to get right back into that muddy slime. Damn Pig!

Anyhow, I got up early and went out to check up on him. Sure as shooting!! I knew this would happen. Let me back up a little to explain the whole scenario. You see, back in Wyoming, when Pork hit it big and was suddenly loaded with Diamonds, the stupid idiot wouldn't keep his big pig trap shut. He went all around town bragging about how rich he was and how he was now in HOG HEAVEN. No more slop for him, and how he will only eat the best of oats and barley, and only the very best of chow from now on. No more dating just any old pig off the street. From now on he was only going to date the very best sows in town.

I kept telling him, keep your big pig trap shut, you're going to get us in trouble, and all he would say is yeah, yeah, yeah. That DAMN PIG!! Big show off, then I said by the way, where did you get all those diamonds? He said, "My motto is Don't Ask Don't Tell, it's a Secret." DAMN PIG! He is always keeping secrets from me. Well long story short. The word gets around real fast around these here parts. And we had Highway Robbers waiting for us here in Montana, just waiting for us to fall asleep so around 1:30 A.M. they decided to go through Pork's bags and while they were doing that it woke Pork up and he starts squealing like the pig that he is and woke up the whole damn neighborhood. Well I always make it a point to unload everything and leave nothing in the bags just in case this might happen. Plus I always make sure the bags are snapped shut, and they were open this morning, and that's what woke Pork up. Those bandits were looking for his diamonds. I told that stupid pig not to brag around town. And I said to him "seeeeeeeee," and he goes "yeah, yeah, yeah." That Damn Pig, is always getting me in trouble.

————◆————

W. Yellowstone, Montana to Boise, Idaho

Day Ten … Who Is That Masked Man.

Well, I see that it's 10:00 A.M. now and I am running late as usual, so I load up the Pork, and hit the trail once more. I ease on to the road and grab a handful of throttle, Pork starts to snort and whine but Silver comes alive and we jump into hyper-drive and ride off into the land of Idaho. (See Photo)

The Lone Rider

Man, I had no idea going into Idaho was going to get me and Pork in so much trouble. Had I known, I would have avoided the whole State. . . . IDAHO, what a diverse state this is, to an extreme sometimes. I will explain as I go through the state, but for now let's just say I am always amazed at how long it takes me to get from one end of the state to the other. I am so used to going across California within a few hours. It's a good thing I can sometimes ride for 10 to 12 hours and get through these states as they are so wide in scope.

As Silver and I descend from high up on Montana's Rocky Mountains and into the valley farm lands of Idaho, we pass so many farms and little towns that if you blink you will miss the town. I am sure that's where the saying comes from. Of course at the speed that Silver and I are traveling it's an easy thing to do. I noticed as we went flying by this little old town, these two old guys sitting in their rocking chairs with their overalls, and straw hats, with a straw sticking out of their mouths, I heard one of them say, "Who is that man with the black mask (My Black Helmet) riding that beautiful hoss? "Why don't you know?" says the other. "That's none other than the Lone Rider and his White Stallion Silver." Just then, in the far distance you could hear. . . . HI-O-SILVER . . . AWAYYYYYY . . .

As Silver and I race across these farm lands you can see way out there in the distance those beautiful Grand Tetons. (See Photo)

Grand Tetons in background and a beautiful valley

They go up as high as 13,766 feet. It's a gorgeous sight from this valley floor. No time to look for long as I have my eyes peeled to the rear view mirrors, at 90 miles an hour I expect old Smokey to come out of some haystack and nail me for sure. It has been a constant struggle trying to figure out what Smokey looks like. Every state that I have gone through has a different type of patrol car. Sometimes they are blue or white, or black and orange, or in a pickup, or an SUV, or station wagon. It's mind blowing. I just don't know what to look for anymore. These country bumpkins might just come out of a haystack in a souped-up tractor with flashing red lights.

Anyhow, on these country roads Silver and I are passing semis as if they are standing still. We passed a semi painted all red, which is unusual as most of them are white or aluminum. I have noticed that I hardly ever see a biker on the road anymore or I see them less and less and when I do see them, they are riding in packs of 6 or 8 or sometimes 12 to 15 in large groups. You do see them riding alone in the cities but out in the open plains hardly ever.

I remember pulling into one of the gas stations a day or two ago and I noticed that every time I pulled in, they stared at me intently. One of them came up and asked me, "Are you riding alone?" "Yep," I said. "Man, you're crazy. Aren't you afraid you'll break down and there won't be anyone around to help you?" "I thought of that," I said, "but I am a lone wolf and I don't follow the pack. I make my own way, I do what I want to do and when I want to, unlike those yahoo's over there who can't agree on what to do because everyone has a different opinion, and no one agrees on anything."

"I can come in here gas up and get out of here in a few minutes while those idiots are still trying to figure it out." "Man, I don't know," he says "you're pretty gutsy to go it alone, especially, out here in the middle of nowhere." "Yeah, I know it's got its good and its bad, but I prefer to go it alone. It's just my style." "See ya, and keep the rubber side down," I said to him, "and be safe." "OK, but I would be afraid to do what you're doing," he said, as I rode off.

As I am speeding down the road I happen to look in my rear view mirror, and holy crap, I see a red light flashing way off in the distance. I pull hard on Silvers reins and we start to bring it down to 55 from 90. I am screwed now. I just knew I would get nailed eventually I thought to myself. As I am staring into the mirror, I noticed that the red light is flashing but it's not coming at me very fast. But the light is getting bigger and bigger. As it got closer, it passed me up and I noticed that it was that damn red semi-truck that we passed awhile ago. The sun was hitting it so that it made it look like a flashing red light. He scared the hell out of me. I thought I was nailed for sure and Pork would have had a field day with that. . . . Damn Pig!

I gave Silver the spurs and off we went like a bat out of hell and up to 90 within a minute. After riding for a couple of hours I pulled into a gas station, ate my apple for the day, had a swig of water and noticed that my canteen was empty. I thought I'd better fill this baby up. I decided to take a shortcut and take Highway 20 through the desert. It's a straight line for Boise Idaho, the capital of the state. It will save me a lot of time, I thought. I had better talk to the man in charge first. He advised me not to. He said, "It's a lonely stretch of desert and no one takes it anymore." Yeah, I thought, but it's one hell of a short cut. (See Map) I got on Pork and I fired him up and all of sudden he starts his usual sputtering and snorting, and choking, and quits. Damn it Pork, not again, so I have to baby him along, until he decides to run. While I am sitting there waiting for him to finish his little tantrum I noticed the red semi-truck that passed us up a while ago, so I moseyed on over and took a picture of it. (See Photo)

The RED BEAST!

Well, Pork finally decided to start and we picked up Highway 20 and head out into the desert. As we ride along I say, "Hey, this is not too bad. It's plenty green out here and things look pretty good." After about two hours into the desert I notice that this has become a desolate place. It's totally devoid of life, and it looks like a godforsaken wasteland. It's totally lifeless, I don't even see a lizard; nothing, not even a tree or cactus. (See Photos)

Vultures looming overhead

What have you got us into?!

Get me the hell out of here!

It is hotter than hell, so I pull over to get a swig of water from my canteen and lo and behold, it's totally empty. Damn it, I remember now, it was empty at the gas station and I was going to fill it up with water and then Pork started to act up and I forgot. "YOU FORGOT!!" squealed Pork, "you forgot, you stupid idiot how could you forget?" "Well it's all your fault," I said. "You started acting up and I had to deal with your little tantrums, so it's your fault." "No, it's your fault," he says. "No it's your fault." I said, "No yours." "No yours." "No yours," we're screaming at each other. When all of a sudden I get this strange feeling like someone is watching us. Meanwhile, Pork is still yelling "It's your fault," etc. (See Photo)

"Shhhhhhhhh," I said, "quiet, I think someone is watching us." "What?" he says. "Yeah, someone is watching us." I start to look around and I don't see anyone, but I still have this strange foreboding feeling that we are being watched.

I climbed up on this rock so I can get a better look around, there is no vegetation that I can see for miles (See Photo) and I can't see anyone. I know someone is watching us, when all of a sudden I see a shadow go by my feet, I jump back because it scared the hell out of me. "Did you see that Pork?" I yelled. "Yeah, I saw it," he squealed. "There it is again," I said "and it looks like its got wings like a plane." Then I look up and to my horror I see it. It's a DAMN vulture flying overhead. "Damn," I said, "how did he know we are out of water?" Those damn vultures have a sixth sense about them, they always know when someone is in deep sh*t. Man, I am screwed now, I say to myself.

Then I heard the vulture say, "Hey boys, come over here, we are having Mexican for dinner tonight." Sure enough within a minute or two there are 5 or 6 of them bast***s flying overhead. "Damn it Pork, I think we are screwed." "What do you mean WE, Kemosabe?" he says, "I don't know if you had noticed but those vultures are Jewish and they don't eat Pork. Oink, Oink, Oink," he is laughing like hell. DAMN PIG!! Well things don't look good here, I am dying of thirst and it's even hotter than before. I need water and I need it bad. (See Photo)

Must find water

I look all around trying to find a solution to my dilemma, when I noticed it, way out in the distance I see it. "It's a lake, it's a lake," I screamed at Pork, "We are saved." I jump on Silver and give him the spurs and we are off and running to the lake. We are at 70, then 80, then 95, now over 100. Who gives a damn? There is no one here but us for miles.

After about 20 minutes of this I pull hard on Silver's reins and we come to a complete stop. What the hell? At the speed we were going we should have been in the middle of the lake by now. It was a mirage, that's what it was, it was just a stupid mirage damn it!! Then all of sudden I saw it again, that shadow, on the ground. I look up and here they are again this time there is about a dozen of them . . . and I scream out in desperation . . . Y . . . ME? . . . Y . . . Y!?

Y--ME?--Y--Y!?

How in the hell did they get here so fast? They must have jets under those wings. Damn vultures! Pork is saying, "Hey, it's not my problem, they don't eat Pork." Damn Pig!

All the while I am hearing Yum-Yum, Mexican dinner tonight boys. Damn Vultures. "WAIT!!!" I said, "I smell something," what says Pork? "Do you smell that?" "Smell what?" he says. It smells like gasoline and the stench of humanity. So, I take off my dark goggles and look around, and then I see it. "I SEE IT—I SEE IT," I yell at Pork. "See what?" he says. "Look over there that green cloud. It's smog, good old smog. I can't wait to inhale that nasty stuff into my clean pure lungs. Hallelujah we are saved! Pork, we are saved!" As I jump on Silver and give him the spurs, as we ride off, I yell at the vultures, "You're not having Mexican tonight, go look for Italian or Chinese, but I warn you if you eat Chinese you'll be hungry in an hour. Ha-ha-ha." And we ride off.

As Silver and I raced toward the puff of green cloud which was still hundreds of miles away, I could barely make it out. But I knew that humanity lived in that obnoxious place and that's where we were heading. It was still many hours away. As we raced toward it I noticed that the landscape was slowly changing and we were starting to see more and more green fields. After a while I was immersed in the most beautiful sight that you can imagine. My God this valley is gorgeous and the mountains and fields are covered in luscious grass and wildflowers. It was so beautiful that I had to stop and take it all in. (See Photo)

Beautiful green pastures and wildflowers

Believe me the photos do not even come close to giving this magical place justice. I stopped and dismounted and just sat there enjoying this wondrous valley. I spent 20 minutes just gazing and breathing in and inhaling the smells of this marvelous place. And this was in the afternoon. I could just imagine how glorious this would be at sunset when the mountains in the background would turn into vivid shades of yellow, then orange, then a light purplish hue.

I mounted up and headed out, but this scenery went on for a very, very long time. It was simply breathtaking. Forget the photo, it does an injustice to this wondrous place. I simply did not want this view to end, but end it did. Remember I had previously mentioned that Idaho was so diverse in scope. I went through some luscious farmlands, then some barren desert, wondrous and beautiful valleys, then hills off in the horizon. WOW! I was so impressed.

Anyhow, as I slowly descended into the sea of humanity, and merged onto Interstate 84 (See Map) on my way to Boise. I was now in three and sometimes four lanes of traffic. People just don't see you and if they do, they just don't give a damn. I constantly had to maneuver in and out of traffic just to stay alive.

My goal was to get through this hellhole and get across and into Oregon as quickly as possible. The traffic was horrendous and the winds in this valley were murderous. Many times I said to myself, "I wish I was back with the vultures, at least I had a fighting chance." As I maneuvered myself into the bowels of the city it started to get worse and worse. I was really tired from being in the desert all this time without water and I had been on the road for many hours now. Pork was squealing that he was hungry and sure enough I looked at his gauge and it was time for his chow. I pulled into the first gas station I saw and I was so beat that I could hardly dismount. My legs hurt and my knees ached, my arms felt like jelly after fighting those horrid winds.

I fed Pork his slop and walked around a bit to get life back into my legs, when I noticed this wanna-be biker pull in. He was riding some huge foreign bike. He pulls his bike right up to me as his stupid stereo is blasting away some stupid rap song. "Hey man where you coming from? I see all your luggage on your Hog." "I'm coming from Sturgis," I said, "Oh, WOW! I always wanted to go there." "What the hell," I thought, "you're just around the corner from the place." Anyhow, he proceeds to show me all the crap he has got on his bike. "Look at this," he says, "I got stereo, and an I-Pod, a GPS and cell phone hooked to my helmet," and, "this bike even has reverse." I thought of telling him, "Damn, why don't you bring your TV with you, you've got everything else, you pansy." But I kept my mouth shut and was polite, because I knew he was clueless. Anyhow, he blurts out, "Hey man, why don't you put a stereo on your Hog?" I said. "No, I like the music my Harley makes. Besides, if he even hiccups I want to know about it."

Anyhow, I bid him goodbye and noticed as I rode away, that he was wishing he had a real bike, like a Harley, instead of that foreign bike "Get a Harley and ride the damn thing," I said to myself. I grabbed a handful of throttle and left that mother in the dust. As I proceeded deeper into the bowels of the city, the traffic got worse and worse. It was now around 5:00 or 5:30 P.M. Have you ever been in L.A. around 5:30 P.M during rush hour? Well, this is Boise, the capital of Idaho and it was a horrendous nightmare. Plus, they were doing road repair. Of course, isn't that the way it always is? They are always working on the damn roads just when you want to get around. It was speed up and then slow down, speed up, then slow down. This went on for miles and miles, it was horrible and very dangerous.

As I inch my way through the city I noticed the enormous Beasts (semi-trucks), are all merging and coming at you from all directions and you don't want to mess with these big guys. You're like a little mosquito to them, a real nuisance. At least out on the freeways or country roads they are either going away from you or they are coming right at you.

Finally we are moving along at a very good pace, when all of a sudden, (all this happens within a minute), I saw red lights suddenly come on all around me and a split second later I smell rubber burning. DAMN!!! I SCREAMED, as I grabbed a handful of brake and immediately stomped on the foot brake and I felt Pork's hoofs dig into the asphalt as we are burning rubber and sliding into the car in front of us. A second before we come to a complete stop I hear the noise of hydraulic air being applied. I quickly look behind me and to my horror I see this huge semi coming right at us. Then I smell rubber and a split second later I see smoke coming out of all of his back tires and he is sliding towards us. And now I focus on the front of his truck and see this giant bloody mouth with huge snarly teeth barreling down on us wanting to devour me and Pork. (I am sure you have seen these giant semis with the huge mouth and teeth painted on their radiators). Well that's what was behind us and coming in to swallow us whole (It reminded me of the movie, JAWS). (Photo)

JAWS

I screamed, "Jump Pork!" as I grabbed a handful of throttle and we bolted to the side of the car in front of us, just as the semi came within a foot of the back of the car. Had we stayed in that spot the truck would not have been able to stop and we would have been pancakes (Well Pork would have been more like sausage). As I looked at the people's faces in the car, their mouths were wide open and you could see the whites of their eyes, they were huge. I am sure they thought that truck was going to do them in. He came damn close to doing it.

I knew had we become road kill, Pork would have gone straight to Hog Heaven, because after all, he has been a good pig, even though I complain a lot about him. But for me, I would have gone straight to hell because I know if I would have gone to the pearly gates and pleaded PAAALLEESEEE, let me in, I didn't mean to break all those speed limits while going through every state. PAAALLLEEESSEE, "Nope," he says, "you're going straight to hell." Oh well, I will give the devil a run for his money . . . heh-heh.

Anyhow, Pork is squealing and screaming at me. "YOU ALMOST GOT US KILLED YOU IDIOT!!! Pay attention you nit-wit," as he is shaking and crying like a little piglet. Well, after that close call I figured I better get us off this interstate. It's really dangerous out here at this time of the day. I told Pork, "Ok, we are going to find and stay in the finest hotel and really treat us right for a change," and he squealed, "It's about time!" Damn Pig, he is never happy.

Well, I found a wonderful hotel with a beautiful plaza right next door. I unloaded the Porker, and took a nice hot shower. Later I went to the plaza for a nice dinner and a great big margarita. When I got back to my room I sat down and looked through some pamphlets regarding the history about Boise. *In May 1833, Captain Benjamin Bonneville's expedition through the present-day city of Boise left a permanent mark on the city's history. Legend states the Frenchmen that accompanied Bonneville famously proclaimed, "Les bois, les bois – voyes les bois (The woods, the woods – see the woods)!" Many believe their observation of the Boise River, at the point where present-day Boise rests, cemented the name of the city forever. The area, however, never garnered much attention. It served as little more than a stopping ground for settlers headed west to Oregon. March 4, 1863, marked a turning point in Idaho and Boise history, when the United States Congress established the Territory of Idaho. On July 5, 1863, Major Pinkney Lugenbeel journeyed through Idaho to found and construct a military outpost, Fort Boise. On July 7, 1863, in the confines of Tom Davis and William R. Ritchie's pioneer cabin, Boise's earliest residents platted the city. Henry Chiles Riggs drew up the plat that included twenty lots and a grid of streets. The city of Boise was born.*

Hotel where Pork and I stayed

Kicking back in my room

Nice plaza

Fountain in the middle

Happy trails

We left Gallatin, Montana at 10:00 A.M. and arrived at our hotel in Boise around 6:00 P.M, an eight hour ride. Tomorrow we head into Oregon. Did we run out of gas in the middle of the desert? You can't miss this!

Until next time,
Joe

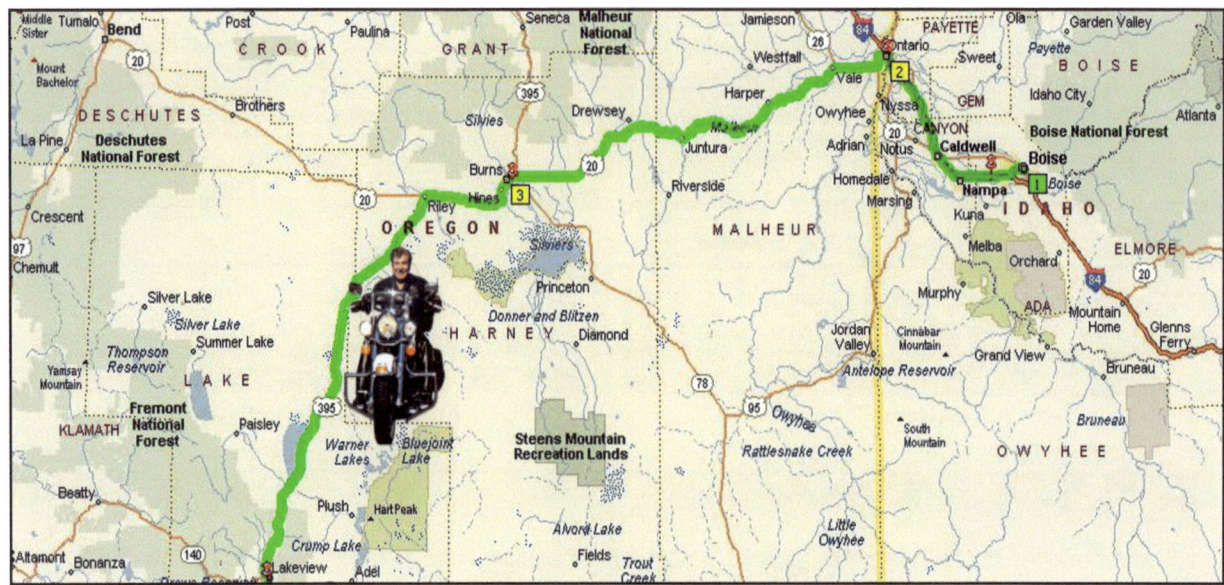

Boise, Idaho to Lakeview, Oregon

Day Eleven … The Point Of No Return

Even though it was a nice hotel, I did not sleep well as the hotel was right next to the freeway and I could hear a steady rush of traffic all night. I got up and left around 8:00 A.M. A very dear friend of mine told me about a very nice place in Oregon, a town named Ashland and my plan was to ride there today.

What a naive little boy am I, I have no concept of distances and perhaps that is why I am able to ride for so many hours, I'm like the Energizer bunny, I just keep going and going and going until it gets dark, then I just find a place to bed down for the night. I am very unhappy that I have not been able to ride at night which I love to do, but the whole idea of making this trip is to see the country.

Ashland, Oregon is one hell of a long way from Boise, Idaho. I don't carry maps, I just rely on the road signs which have served me well through my many travels, like taking advice from those Indians earlier, surrreeeeee. But unlike most men, I am not adverse to asking for directions, matter of fact I go out of my way to pick the brains of the locals about the road ahead.

Anyhow, Silver and I are racing down the freeway at incredible speeds and I, of course am looking for Smokey. I wonder what they look like in these parts of the woods. We are moving so fast and I got my eyes peeled to my rear view mirrors, that I miss my turnoff. "DAMN!" Now I have to double back. I had to ride down the freeway a few miles before I could turn around, come back and get back on the freeway again and take the right turn off. Oh well, such is life, not like I have not done that before. Hell, I can't do everything and still look for the cops. Finally we enter Oregon. (See Photo)

Oregon here we come

What are we doing out here?!

Pork says, I want to go home

I was warned that the eastern part of the state was pretty barren and believe me some parts were. However, we did pass through many beautiful valleys and farms, but these were parts of Oregon that were still very close to Idaho. My plan was to take 20 out of Boise drop down to 395, then 140 into Medford, then Ashland. However, as you all know, nothing is always as simple as it seems. I had been riding Highway 20 all the way from Yellowstone and if you want to see what this country really looks like, that's the road to take.

Now the landscape is turning barren and it's becoming hotter and hotter and there is less vegetation. I am now entering into no man's land (See Map) and there are hardly any cars on the road. Now we are totally isolated and gas stations are very few and far between.

Miles and miles of endless road

I decided that instead of going north to Bend, Oregon, I would take 395, go south, and then go west through Dead Indian Memorial Road and on up to Ashland. (See Map) I had no idea how isolated and remote this stretch of road was. If I had to do it all over again I would not take this road, not even in a car because there were no cars taking this route. The locals knew better. Prior to entering this no man's land I stopped and got fuel at a little gas station in the middle of nowhere, it had one gas pump. (See Photo)

One gas pump station

Oh, on another matter, in Oregon you're not allowed to pump your own gas, an attendant has to hand you the pump in order for you to do it. It's totally crazy. Ladies would love it!

But I digress, I asked the people at the station about my route of travel. They told me that it was barren and isolated and no one really traveled it, but it was one hell of a short cut to Ashland. I asked them about fuel along my route and the lady said that there was a gas station half way through the desert, but that she had not been through there in some time. Well a gas station half way through made sense to me and I decided to go for it. The sign says "Rough Road" and you can believe every word of it. (See Photo)

Point of no return

Down into the Valley of Doom we proceeded, Pork, Silver and I. It starts to get hotter than hell and dust storms everywhere, I am now running on a little past half empty and I am getting really nervous, and Pork is screaming, "Hey, I'm getting hungry here." I am straining to see into the horizon for that gas station, but there is none in sight, so we keep barreling on down the road hoping to eventually find it. When finally off into the distant horizon I see a little speck of what looks like a building and I yell at Pork, "We're safe, you'll get food." Damn Pig! Finally we arrive at the building and it's a ghost town. Spider webs all over the windows and doors, you could tell no one has been in this building for a very long time. There is a sign on the old rusted out gas pump that says 'look for a red truck ten miles down the road for fuel.'

I am extremely upset and very nervous about this whole state of affairs. I am at the point of no return. I cannot go back because it's farther to go back than to try and make Lakeview, which is the closest town on the other side of this God forsaken stretch of road. Aliens from outer space could build a colony here and no one would notice. Well, I am now committed to going forward, so we press forward with the hopes of finding that elusive red truck.

After more than ten miles, I conclude that there is no red truck and that sign was pretty damn old to begin with. Who knows how long ago it was put there? That might have been a year ago for all I know. I stopped and got off Pork and thought, now what? I have a very long way to go and my fuel situation is critical.

While sitting there I noticed way off in the distance what appeared to be a building. My hopes were high again and I jumped on Pork and headed down the road toward the building. Upon arriving I noticed that it was a government building of some kind and there was a trailer, which appeared to me that someone lived there. The place had a fence all around it but the gate was open. I revved Pork's pipes real loud hoping to attract someone's attention, but no one responded. I did not want to go onto someone's private property but these were desperate times. I got off Pork and started to go through the gate when I noticed a large stake in the ground with a long chain attached to it.

"Oh-oh, a dog lives here," I said to myself, "What to do?" I had no choice, I had to go forward to the trailer. But first I best get some protection on me before going in. So I went back to Pork and put on my heavy gloves and chaps and jacket, it was so hot I could barely get it on me. The leather was practically burning me but I thought if there is a dog and he comes at me at least I have some measure of protection. I approached the trailer very carefully all the while yelling, "HELLO – HELLO," no one answered. Finally I made it to the trailer and I could hear a fan running in the trailer, so I started banging on the door and still no one answered. By this time I figured there is no dog or he would have been on my throat by now. I walked all around the trailer yelling, 'HELLO.' It was my conjecture that no one was at home, I made every attempt to arouse someone. I went back to Pork fired him up and drove him through the gate right up to a pickup.

I figured I would use my Oklahoma Credit Card (hose) and help myself to a couple of gallons of fuel. That was all I needed to make it back to civilization. And I would leave a few bucks to pay for it. As I proceeded to stick the hose into the gas tank, DAMN IT ANYHOW!!! If it isn't one of those new cars that won't allow you to stick a hose into them, it is a measure of keeping someone like me from stealing gas. Damn! I was willing to pay for it. I am not a thief!

At this point I have no choice but to continue down the road and hope that I can make it across this wasteland. After a few miles of traveling down this foreboding land of the devil, I notice a building way in the horizon. "Ah, we are safe," I yell at Pork. "Sure I heard that before," he mumbles. When I finally got to the location, I noticed that it is a shack with a small bathroom and a drinking fountain. OK, I get off Pork and size up my situation. I can stay here, where there is water and a bathroom, or I can chance it and go for it and maybe make Lakeview over 50 miles away. I am pretty sure I can make it but there are a lot of up and down hills along the way and the wind is blowing straight into me. "Hmmmm, if I go for it and run out of fuel I will be stuck out there in the middle of the desert with no water or bathroom, etc." While contemplating my dilemma I noticed a dot way off in the distance and as I strained to get a better look I saw that it was a car. I yell at Pork, "We are saved, a car is coming!" "Sure," he says, " I've heard that before." Damn Pig!

Anyhow, I grab the Oklahoma Credit Card (a hose) and step out into the road and start waving it at the car, and I hear this woman screaming at her husband, "Don't stop, don't stop. Can't you see it's a Mexican Bandito. He's wearing a black mask. Step on the gas, hurry, step on the gas. I know he is going to rob, pillage and rape me." As they sped away, I was yelling, "Sure, in your wildest dreams you ugly, fat cow. No one would rape you if you were the last woman on the planet." I was screaming "Come back you dumb idiots. I have an Oklahoma Credit Card." "Nice going," says Pork, "You're a real charmer." "Oh shut up you old Pig."

Anyhow, after a while I see another dot in the horizon. "Seeeeeee," I tell Pork. "We have another chance." And he says, "Yeah well, don't blow it this time." Anyhow, this nice looking pickup comes into view and he pulls into the spot where we are, and before I can say a word, he jumps out of his truck and runs into the bathroom. Meanwhile, I'm standing there holding my Oklahoma Credit Card. He finally comes out and I said, "I will pay for just a couple of gallons of gas." "Well I don't know," he said, "I am kind of low on fuel myself." "I just need about a gallon just to make sure I can get across this desert." "Well, ok," he said. So I stick the hose into his tank and damn if the thing will not go in. It's another one of those new trucks that block the use of the hose. "DAMN IT!!" I scream. "Well, it's too bad buddy. I wish I could help you." "That's alright," I said. "At least you were generous enough to offer."

As he drives off, I hear Pork say, "Now what, genius?" Damn Pig! "We wait," I said. Soon after, I see another dot in the horizon, and I say to Pork, "Seeeeeee," "Yeah, sure," he responds. Soon, a beat up old pickup shows up and they pull in. It's an old lady and an old man. I explain my situation and they gladly offer to help. In the meantime, I had already gathered some old plastic bottles from the dumpster and was ready to siphon some gas. "I just need a couple of gallons," I said, and she said, "We travel these parts all the time, we're rock collectors." I am thinking, "Hmmmm, that's against the law. You're not allowed to take rocks from a national park," but who am I to question these nice folks. I said "I know you're not rock collectors!" They were shocked I said that. "WHAT?" they said. I told them, "You are my Angels." I said, "You just saved me from being stuck out here in the middle of nowhere." I just took a gallon of gas and offered to pay them for it. They would not take the money and told me to pass it on. Little did they know that I have saved many a motorist in distress in my travels, as well. I asked "How far to Lakeview?" She replied "A little over 50 miles." I said, "Adios," and hit the road, they were going the opposite way.

Sure enough just as I had predicted, there were many hills and strong headwinds and it was chewing up my gas real quick. I was cussing myself for being so stupid for not taking more gas when they offered it, but I did not want to take advantage of them. But now, I'm sweating bullets and by the time I hit Lakeview I was biting my nails and sucking fumes.

When I got to this little one horse town, (where if you blink you would probably miss it) it did have a flea bitten motel and a gas station. So the first thing I did was feed Pork and went into the motel. "EIGHTY FIVE DOLLARS!! I SCREAMED! But, but, but, WHYYYYYYYYYY? For just a bed and a shower?" "Yep," the old hag says, "and it's the last room we have, take it or leave it." "Yeah, I heard that line before," I thought to myself. "Why so much I asked?" "Because they are laying a gas line through the desert, it's a government project and we have men staying here that work the gas line. So we can get that kind of money because the government pays it. Do you want the room or not?" "Do I have a choice?" I am thinking. I have been on the road since Boise, and almost stuck in the desert.

I have been on the road since 8 A.M. and it is now about 7:00 or 7:30 P.M., almost 12 hours of hard riding. Hell, I didn't tell the old lady this, but I would have paid her a $100 bucks just to grab a bed and shower. I didn't go out to eat that night, I had not eaten for 12 hours and I don't know why, but I was not hungry. Perhaps it was the heat outside, I don't know but I just took a shower and hit the sack and went to sleep.

Good Night,
Joe

Lakeview, Oregon to Ashland, Oregon

Day Twelve … A River Runs Through It

I slept well that night but woke up sore all over, it's now about 6:30 A.M. and time to get out of Dodge. I took a shower and WHAT!!! No coffee pot. Damn, for the price I paid for this dump I should have had coffee brought to me in bed. Oh, now I remember the old hag telling me there would be coffee and donuts in the lobby, what lobby? It was more like a one room closet. Oh-oh, I just remembered her telling me that this motel was loaded with guys that work the pipe line, I better get my butt down there quick before they drink all the coffee and eat up all the donuts, I am really hungry now.

Well I get dressed and run down there to get my cup of Java, WHAAATTT!!! 'There are no donuts?' "Nope," she says, "you're too late, they ate it all." Damn. "But it's only 7:30 A.M." I said, "You should have gotten here earlier," she said. Oh well, you can't argue with these country bumpkins, but I did manage to get one cup of coffee, thank God. So I go down to load up Pork, "Huh? Who? What? What?" Apparently I woke Pork from a sound sleep. "What's up, where we going?" he says. "I don't know" I said. "Whichever way the wind is a blowing, maybe up over them thar mountains." "Oh boy, there he goes with that Bull Sh*t again. In case you forgot we are going to Ashland you nitwit," he says. Damn Pig! Thinks he knows everything.

Anyhow, a little bit of history on Lakeview: *The Town of Lakeview, established in 1876 is the county seat of Lake County Oregon. With an elevation of 4798 feet, Lakeview is often referred to as the "Tallest Town in Oregon". Lakeview is situated at the foot of the Warner Mountains and at the edge of the southeast Oregon High Desert. The site of Lakeview was donated by M.W. Bullard who settled in Goose Lake Valley in 1869. The town was first known as Bullard's Ranch or Bullard's Creek. This name gave way to Lakeview because of the excellent view of Goose Lake that was seen from the town site at the time. Lakeview became the county seat of Lake County (which then also comprised the area of what is now Klamath County) a general election held in November of 1876, winning over Lakeview (later Klamath Falls) by a vote of 242 to 181. After being established in 1876, Lakeview grew as a commercial center for area sheep and cattle ranches. Lakeview continues to be a business center for the region, with agriculture and lumber now serving as the main industries. Lakeview has always been the center of a large trading area and is the natural location for a town, nestled as it is against the hills on the east and the great open valley on the west. Lakeview is on the border of the last frontier and referred to as Oregon's Outback.*

Well I loaded up the Pork and left about 8:00 A.M. I had not eaten anything all day yesterday and only had a cup of coffee this morning, so I looked for a restaurant on my way out of town but did not see any. I figured oh well, it's only a two and half hour ride to Klamath Falls. I will grab a bite there. I picked up highway 140 and headed West. After about a half hour we started to come across some very beautiful valleys, and then I noticed it, (See Map) a beautiful river that runs right through the valley and flows right along the road for hundreds of miles. (See Photo)

A beautiful river that runs for miles and miles

I was so mesmerized by the river that it almost got me killed on a number of occasions. I am very partial to rivers as I used to build canoes and kayaks just for fun and I still have the canoe that I built about 35 years ago. I have shot almost every river in California; the American, the Russian, the Sacramento, the Stanislaus and many, many others in my kayak and canoe. I have even been out in the ocean with both. When I saw this beautiful river I just went wild with anticipation of someday returning here and shooting this lovely river which would carry me for hundreds of miles, all the while camping along its shores. I just can't wait. God, please let me live long enough to come and meander along this peaceful valley and just flow along with the river; it is calling me and I can't wait to return.

I was so taken by it that it nearly killed me. I came damn close to just running off the road, because I just couldn't help but stare at it. After a long while the river disappeared, thank God, because it would have gotten me killed eventually. Anyhow, we arrived in the city of Klamath Falls. I pulled into a gas station and fed Pork his chow. And as usual, there are a bunch of bikers hanging around the gas station trying to figure out what to do with themselves, when this old timer comes up to me and says "Hi; where you coming from?" "Sturgis," I said. "Wow, you've come a long way." "Well, I'm actually from California," I said. "Wow, that's even more impressive," he said. "Where you headed?" "Ashland." "Oh, my, my, you still have a long way to go." "Yep, but I'm a lot closer than I was before." "Have a nice ride and be safe," he said as he drove out of sight.

Well, I must have gotten something to eat some place somewhere, but I really don't remember now. But one thing that I do, is keep the receipts of every gas stop and restaurant and motel that I stay at. That way I have proof of my travels and I can relive my experience as I put it all in perspective later on. The receipts have the time and date and address of everywhere I have been and it's easy to remap everything. One thing I have noticed during my many travels on Pork is that when I am at the gas station feeding Pork, almost without exception someone will come up and talk to me, whether it is men, women, or children. They see my luggage and they know I'm on the road, and they feel compelled to come and talk to me. I believe it's the single fact that I'm a lone rider and they are not intimidated by me as they are by the group of bikers whom they seem to avoid. I've seen this scenario played out many, many times in my travels. That is why I'm able to talk to the locals about their towns, the roads and the best way to get out of Dodge. It's interesting that a pack of bikers seems to spell trouble in the mind of many, but a single biker says "adventurous."

I remember, just a few days ago when I was going through the state of Wyoming, I pulled into this little hick town to feed Pork (as usual). I noticed (as usual) a group of bikers, they always seem to ride in packs, (I know that it's to watch out for each other in case of trouble). But I make my own way, that's my style. As I was feeding the Porker, this lady came out of the store, came up to me and gave me a big hug. "Hi" she says, "and Welcome to Wyoming." I said, "Well thank you." And she proceeded with the usual, "Where you going? Where you coming from? How's the ride?" She proceeded to tell me that she was born there and she loves her little town and that her husband works in the mines and her children are in high school, etc. Then she says, "Well, have a nice ride and be safe." I said, "Thank you and take care of yourself." Then this biker guy comes up to me and says, "Do you know that lady?" I said "No." "WOW! She sure was friendly," he said. "Oh that," I said, "that happens to me all the time." He gives me a funny look as I ride off. I would have explained it to him, but since he rides with a pack, he is clueless and would not have understood what I was talking about.

Anyhow, I digress, let's get back to Klamath Falls. After feeding the Pork I fire him up, took off and about three blocks down the road he starts pulling his old crap again, sputtering, choking, spitting, and making a scene. So I baby talk to him and tell him what a good little pig he is and how much I appreciate him and all that crap. Anyhow he falls for it and off we go. We cross the

Klamath River and head into the Redwoods. It reminds me so much of Santa Cruz, California it made me feel right at home. (See Photos)

Klamath River

Into the Redwoods

A half an hour later we descended into a beautiful valley and I eased back on Silver's reins and started to relax, when all of a sudden I get hit with a 45 caliber bullet (big bug) and it hits me so hard it almost knocks me off the saddle and man, does it hurt. It hit me right on the ribs and it stings like a bee sting. A few minutes later I get hit with machine gun fire and man I am covered with bug juice all over, boots, chaps, jacket; man, you should see me, (maybe you'd better not see me as I'm not a pretty sight, you might puke). If you don't believe me, check out the Photos.

Off the bike

On the bike

This happens to me quite a bit throughout my trip, especially going through these very fertile valleys; there are a lot of bugs there getting their fill of food.

Well when I arrive at Keno, I stop at a gas station and give Pork some more slop. I am thinking, "Damn, he's going to give me a bad time again, I just know it," when a stranger steps up and said, "Hey, where you going, where you coming from?" Honest this happens almost always. I tell him that I'm at the crossroads here; I'm not sure whether to take Dead Indian Road or Highway 66 and cut across the Hayden Mountain Pass. (See Map) "Oh no," he says, "you've got to go over the pass. It's a beautiful ride. I know because I have a motorcycle and I've done it." "Oh yeah," I said, "What have you got?" "I have a . . . (foreign bike)." And he quickly added, "BUT IT LOOKS LIKE A HARLEY!!" All of a sudden I heard Pork mumbling to himself, I knew what he was saying but I kept it to myself. "I'll take your advice and take the pass." I thanked him and of course Pork pulled the same crap again so I had to baby talk to him again; Spoiled Pig.

After about a five hour ride we finally arrived in Ashland. I rode through town checking it all out when I see a Best Western. "Hmmmm", we haven't stayed in a Best Western so far, so I told Pork, "We're stopping here." He was glad to hear it.

"WHAAAAAT!!! YOU HAVE GOT TO BE KIDDING ME!!!..ONE HUNDRED AND EIGHTY FIVE DOLLARS. . . . WHYYYYYY?" What's the reason this time for an overpriced room? "Because it's August and it's the Shakespeare festival here in Ashland." "But I don't like Shakespeare, I don't even understand what they're saying, what with their Hark, where art thou, Juliet, crap." "It's still $185 a night." "Hmmmm, I think I will pull, the old, OH LOOK AT POOR PORK. . . . " So I start with. . . . "But, but, but, look at poor Pork he is so tired and all dirty." "Soooo," she says, "it's still $185 a night." Man that woman was as cold as a witches T**, well you know what I mean. Anyhow I go and get on Pork, and he goes, "Huh, what, what, where we going?" "Never mind," I said. I go up the street about 6 blocks and spot a very nice looking motel called the Flagship Inn. (See Photos)

Motel we stayed at **The view from my bike**

I go in and ask about the rate and he says seventy-two bucks a night. I say, "Now that's what I am talking about. For that price Pork and I are staying here for two nights, as to the one night at the other place." The room was clean, with a nice bathroom, and clean sheets. Ok, I am a happy camper and Pork is in Hog Heaven because he gets to rest. I take a shower get cleaned up and walk across the street where there is a Mexican Restaurant. The clerk said it was good food. I order a Margarita and some chow and kick back and people-watch, my favorite thing to do. Afterward I go back to my room and write up this note and plan on tomorrow's walkabout. One photo is without me on Pork and one with me on Pork, just in case you don't believe me about the bugs. (Photos)

Tomorrow, the Porker falls in love and makes his play on a cute little redhead. You can't miss that. *"Get your motor running, head out on the highway, looking for adventure and whatever comes our way Born to be Willllddd" . . . oh, yeah, now were're talking.

Good Night,
Joe

Day Thirteen ... PorkChop's Cute Little Redhead

Well yesterday was about a five hour ride, short ride by our standards, so I got up pretty well rested, showered, and went to the continental breakfast that the motel was serving. Got coffee and a bowl of cereal, and I was fine with the world. The weather was perfect, clear blue skies, not a cloud in the sky and it was nice and comfortable outside. I put on a short sleeve shirt and grabbed the camera and went out to Pork and said, "Guess what? I am not going to load you up with luggage this time, we're just going out to look around. We are just going to do the tourist thing and ooooh and ahhhh and take pictures." "Alright," he says, "No more baggage to carry, I like it!"

So I mounted up and off we go. We rode up and down the streets just looking and getting the lay of the land when I saw a nice little park and decided to go take a look and take some pictures. I rode around, until I found a good spot for Pork to hang out while I went to take some pictures. As I was parking him, this guy walked by and I asked him if he wouldn't mind taking a picture of me and the bike. I did not say Pork or anything like that because he would have called the Nut Wagon to pick me up. Hey, you guys know what I mean if you've been reading my memos, you know I'm wacko. He said, "No problem," and took the photo of me hanging out with the Pork. (See Photo)

Out on the town

Waiting for a two wheeler

Anyhow, just as I was putting things away, the Pork starts yelling "GET OUT OF HERE!! GET OUT OF HERE!!" I go "What? What?" He says, "Go across the street." I go, "WHY?" And he says, "Because you see that cute little two wheel redhead coming this way?" I go, "Yeah, so?" "Well if you stay here you're going to spoil my action, NOW GET!" I go, "Ok, Ok," Damn Pig! As I go across the street, old Pork starts whistling at the cute little two wheeler and to my surprise she moseys on over to him and stops. Then Pork starts laying a bunch of Hogwash on her as I take the picture. (See Photo)

PorkChop's cute little red head

After seeing those two together I decided to leave them alone and take a nice leisurely stroll through this lovely little town. (See Photos) Finally I spotted a cozy little restaurant overlooking a beautiful babbling brook and decided to have lunch there.

Downtown Ashland

An inspirational moment

Babbling brook

Here's to you

Finally a waitress comes by and seats me right next to a table with three women and I can hear every word they were saying. Since I had no one with me, and I was not distracted, I could hear their total conversation. They were talking about their husbands and boyfriends and on and on. It was worse than Sex and the City type stuff and I would tell you all about what they said but it's too graphic to discuss in public. I was totally blushing just too much for my ears.

By this time two hours had passed, and I thought I better get back to Pork because we only had two hours on the meter. As I came around the corner, lo and behold if the cute little two wheeler redhead was still there snuggled right in his pig pen (Parking Spot). As I start to walk up to him I could hear him telling her all about his travels and about how he almost got eaten by some vultures etc. So I went up to him and said, "I thought you said they didn't eat pork." And he goes, "Shhhhhhhh, go away. You're spoiling my action. I am about a hogs hair from scoring here, go away!!" "Nope," I said, "We are going, time's up." "Noooooooo," he says squealing his lungs out. "I am making progress here, I am almost to home plate. Pleeessseeee, I know she is crazy about me!" "Yeah, Yeah, I heard this before, let's go." "Noooooooo." He's squealing all the way back.

Well, I get back to the motel and park the Porker. I know he is totally upset with me now and he probably won't start tomorrow just to get even. Oh, well I will deal with it then. I had planned on going to a nice restaurant for dinner, but after walking around town I realized how tired I was. I was not used to walking, I was only used to riding so I was bushed and didn't go out, just hit the sack.

Good Night, You All...

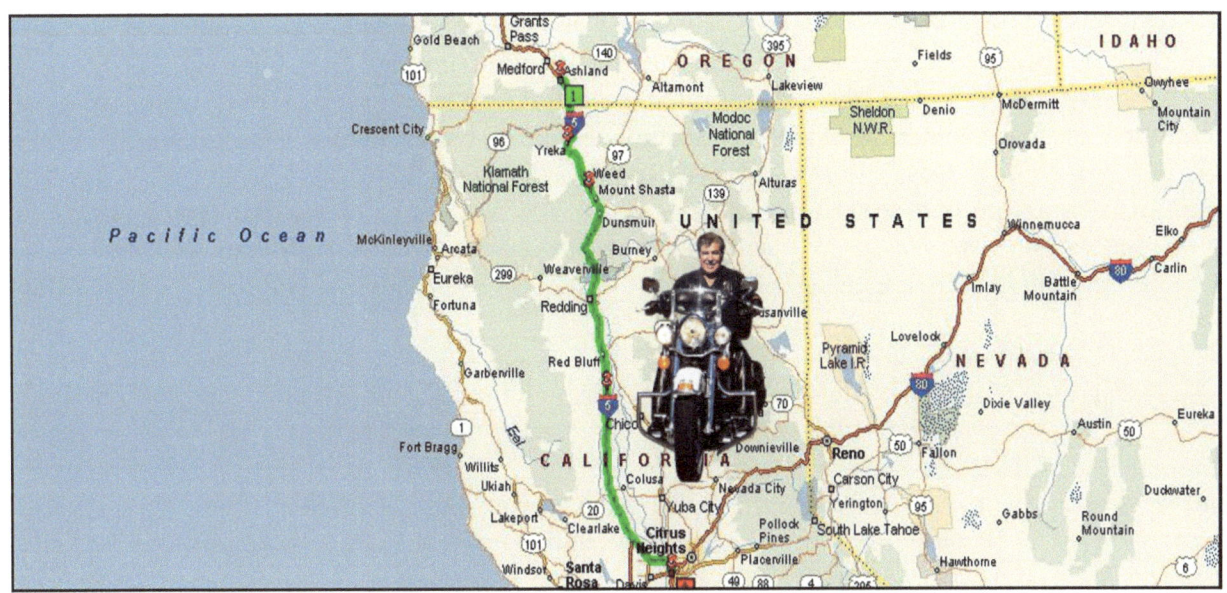

Ashland, Oregon to Sacramento, California

Day Fourteen … Memory Lane

I got up nice and rested, but my feet hurt from all that walking. I went to the lobby and got some coffee and something to snack on, then went back to my room to look up a bit of history on Ashland: *Prior to the arrival of settlers in mid-1800s, Shasta Indians lived in the valley along the creek approximately where Ashland is located. Early Hudson's Bay Company hunters and trappers, following the Siskiyou Trail, passed through the site in the 1820s. In the late 1840s, settlers (mostly American) following the Applegate Trail began passing through the area. By the early 1850s, the Donation Land Act brought many white settlers into the Rogue Valley and in conflict with its native people. These often- violent clashes continued until 1856.*

Gold was discovered near Jacksonville in 1851, contributing to the influx of settlers. Several men arrived to camp in what is now the Ashland area in January of 1852: Abel Helman, Eber Emery and his brother James, Robert Hargadine and others. In order to capitalize on mining in nearby Jacksonville, Helman and the Emerys established a lumber mill on Ashland Creek (then called Mill Creek). During the 1860s and 1870s the community grew, establishing a school, churches and other businesses. In 1871 the Post Office dropped "Mills" from Ashland's name. The following year Reverend Skidmore founded the Ashland Academy--it eventually became Southern Oregon University. Ashland is well known for its annual Oregon Shakespeare Festival (OSF), which brings thousands of visitors to the city every year. The festival has grown from a summer outdoor festival in the 1930s to a season, which stretches from February to October, incorporating Shakespeare and non-Shakespearean plays in repertory at three theaters. The Ashland City Band is the oldest continuous city band in the United States.

I decided it was time to leave so I went out and told Pork that we were leaving. "LEAVING?" HE SQUEALS AS LOUD AS HE CAN. "NOOOOOOO, PAAALLLEEESE TAKE ME BACK

TO TOWN!!!" I go, "Why?" He says, "I want to see if I can find that cute little two wheeling redhead. I know she loves me. I was as close as my chinny-chin-chin from scoring. I was making total progress until you came along and spoiled my action." "Hey," I said "You're going on and on about the little two wheeler, what about them three wheelers I see all around the freeways?" (Three Wheel Motorcycles) "Hey," he says, "Have you seen their back end? They're huge, they got big butts. I am totally not into those fat mamas." "That's too bad, we're hitting the trail." "Where we going?" he asks. "I am not sure," I said, "whichever way the wind is a blowing, maybe up over them thar mountains." "Oh man," I hear him say, "there he goes with that Bull Sh** again. What a nit-wit."

So I walk over to the grass and grab a handful of it and toss it in the air and watch it float down. "Well, "I say," the wind is a-blowing south, so Partner, looks like that's the way we are a-heading." "GREAT!!" he squeals. "That's the way home, it's about time. But PAAALLLEEESE, can we go back to town just for a little bit? I know she is waiting for me." I go, "Nope, we're hitting the trail." "Damn it," he says, "You're just jealous because women have not even looked at your ugly face on this whole trip."

"OH YEAH!!" I snapped back at him, "What about all those women over there crying their eyes out because I am a-leaving?" "WHAT WOMEN?" He asks. "Those women across the street, over yonder; can you hear them? They are crying and weeping and saying. "Don't Go, Lone Rider, Don't Go, Pleassseee don't go, we'll miss you Lone Rider."

I told Pork, "I am going to go over there and talk to them poor weeping little ladies." So I mosey on over and say, "Don't cry little darlings, I'll be back someday, look for me coming back over yonder, from them thar mountains, look for me and my old hoss, Silver and my trusty sidekick, PorkChop. We will return someday, just wait for me." "WAIT FOR YOU!!! WAIT FOR YOU!!!" I hear Pork shout and say, "In your wildest dreams they'll wait for you. WHAT AN IDIOT!" Oink, oink, oink, I hear him laughing. "Oh shut up," I say to him and then I mount up and ride off into the sunset. Well technically it's still morning but you get my drift.

P.S. Off the record, have you ever looked at something and said, "Wow, that would be a great shot," and you did not take the photo? Well that happened to me and I could kick myself over and over again. When I came around the corner and saw a cute little red Moped parked in the same spot as Pork. I thought Ahhh, how cute is that. and DAMN IT!!! I did not take the shot. It would have been a wonderful photo worth framing. A Great Kodak moment. Dammmmn It!

OK, back to Pork and the idiot, not me, the other idiot. Wheeeee, I hear Silver, Oh, oh, he is not happy. And now we're hitting the trail and heading south, back to Pork's Pig Pen. But something happens along the way. Stay tuned.

Ride on Lone Rider. Ride on... poor little ladies that I left behind . . . "Yeah, sure, in your dreams," says Pork . . . Damn Pig!

As we hit the trail and leave Oregon behind we enter into California. (See Photos)

We are leaving Oregon

Ahhhhh, California

I could feel Silver's legs grow stronger and stronger under me. His gait became faster and faster until he hit his stride and we were once again at his usual 90 mph. I knew he was anxious to get back to his stall and the little mare he had left behind. "HI-O-SILVER," I said to him and off we went barreling down I-5. (See Map)

Now we're merging into three and sometimes four lanes of traffic and of course, I have my eyes peeled on the mirrors. At least I know what to look for now that we are in California, the old Black and White, the CHP, (California Highway Patrol). Somewhat comforting, but not always, as they pull a switch-a-roo on you sometimes. The traffic was horrible, what with the Beast and Cages all around us just waiting for us to make a false move so they can run us over. I had this strange longing to be back in the desert again, at least there the only things that can get you are the vultures, heh-heh, not Pork of course.

All of a sudden, Mt. Shasta comes into view; man, what a sight! We had to stop and do a photo shoot. (See Photo)

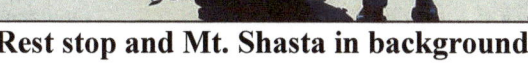

Rest stop and Mt. Shasta in background

Mt. Shasta

Besides, Silver needed a rest and as soon as we came to a stop Pork started whining about going back to see his little two wheeler…. Damn Pig!

Anyhow, I mounted up and hit the trail. I gave Silver the spurs and he bolted out and man, he hit 90 and within a few minutes we come up on a sign that says, 65 mph. What the hell! Do they want us to get out and walk? We'll never get there at that speed, so I let Silver do his thing and man he is going like a bat out of hell. Of course, I have my face glued to the mirrors and keenly watch for the law. WHEN ALL OF A SUDDEN I see him! A Black and White and he is barreling down behind me, lights a-flashing,

DOES HE NAIL ME?

DO I FINALLY GET MY JUST DESSERTS? (Which I truly deserve, by the way.)

STAY TUNED . . . NAW, I'M JUST KIDDING. I WOULDN'T DO THAT TO YOU!

I immediately start to think of an excuse, PAAALLLEEESSE, hos-a-fer, I didn't mean to do it, the Pork made me. Snort, Snort I hear him grumbling. Finally, "you're going to get it you idiot," he says. Anyhow, I pull hard on Silvers reins and he doesn't want to stop, he wants to get back to his stall. I pull even harder and then he starts to slow down. Suddenly, the Black and White shoots right by me and pulls over a cage that was a few cages in front of me. Poor guy, I feel for him. As I went by I could hear him saying, "But officer, he was going faster than me," as he points directly at me. "You fink," I say to myself.

Well Pork is squealing that he is hungry, so I pull off the trail and feed him his slop, and notice a hamburger joint. "Hmmmm," I haven't had slop in quite a while, just healthy food, like apples etc.

So I park the Pork and mosey on over and order up some chow. I am sitting there looking out the window enjoying my grub and keeping an eye on Pork, when I notice this couple looking him over and walking all around him. They finally come in and order up something, "Nice bike" he says, "Thanks." "Where are you coming from and where are you going?" "I'm coming from Sturgis." "Oh, I have been there a couple of times and I have a Harley as well." "Oh," I said as I get all excited, finally a fellow Hog rider to talk to.

"Did you ride your Hog there all the way he asks?" "Yep," I said. "Did you ride yours there as well?" "Naw," he said. "I trailered it." "YOU TRAILERED YOUR HOG THERE?" I SCREAMED! "The only time you put your hog on a trailer is when he is sick and you need to take him to the hospital," I screamed. That is a total insult to your Hog man! A Harley must be ridden, not trailered. What's the matter with you? You namby pamby. Then his wife or girlfriend chimed in and said, "Well big deal. Where else have you ridden besides Sturgis?" She acted as though I was a beginner. "Do you really want to know?" I asked, "Sure," she says, sarcastically.

The gauntlet had been thrown. "Well let me seeeeeee. For starters of course there is:

California,
Nevada,
Arizona,
Mexico,
Utah,
Oklahoma,
New Mexico,
Texas,
Kansas,
Illinois,
Wisconsin,
Indiana,
Ohio,
Pennsylvania,
New Jersey,
Missouri,
Nebraska,
Colorado,
So. Dakota,
Wyoming,
Montana,
Idaho,
Oregon and
New York

I went to all those places, by myself, no buddies, no other bikers, just me and my Hog. And I have restaurant and gas receipts to prove I have been there." Her mouth dropped with amazement and she did not say another word the whole time after that. I finally bid them farewell and told him, "Ride that Harley, Dude."

I mounted Pork and said, "Let's get the hell out of here, that guy is a trailer queen." We hit the trail once again and Silver jumped into hyper-drive and off we went. After awhile, we got into Redding and later Red Bluff and of course stupid me, we ended up riding right in the middle of the afternoon. Man, did we take a beating for miles and miles, of relentless, furious hot winds. My plan was to ride all the way home, a 7 or 8 hour ride, easy by our standards. As we started to approach Sacramento, nostalgic memories started to set in and I decided to stop and stay overnight and visit some of my old stomping grounds. I used to live there and my children were born there, except my youngest, he was born in Santa Cruz.

Anyhow, I thought it would be fun. So I decided to stay overnight. I pulled into the first Motel 6 that I saw and SCREAMED, "$37 DOLLARS!! ARE YOU KIDDING ME? Man, I thought; WOW! This is the cheapest rate of the whole trip. "I'll take it," I yelled. The room was clean, nothing special, just a place to bed down for the night. I unloaded Pork, took a shower and went out to Old Town for dinner. I had not been there in many years. (See Photos)

Out on the town

Old Town Sacramento

He is stoned drunk

Trying to wake him

Well after having a nice steak dinner and a glass of good wine, I decided to hang out with my buddies but they got so drunk that I had to leave. I had a long ride home tomorrow and I needed to hit the sack.

Hasta Luego,
Joe

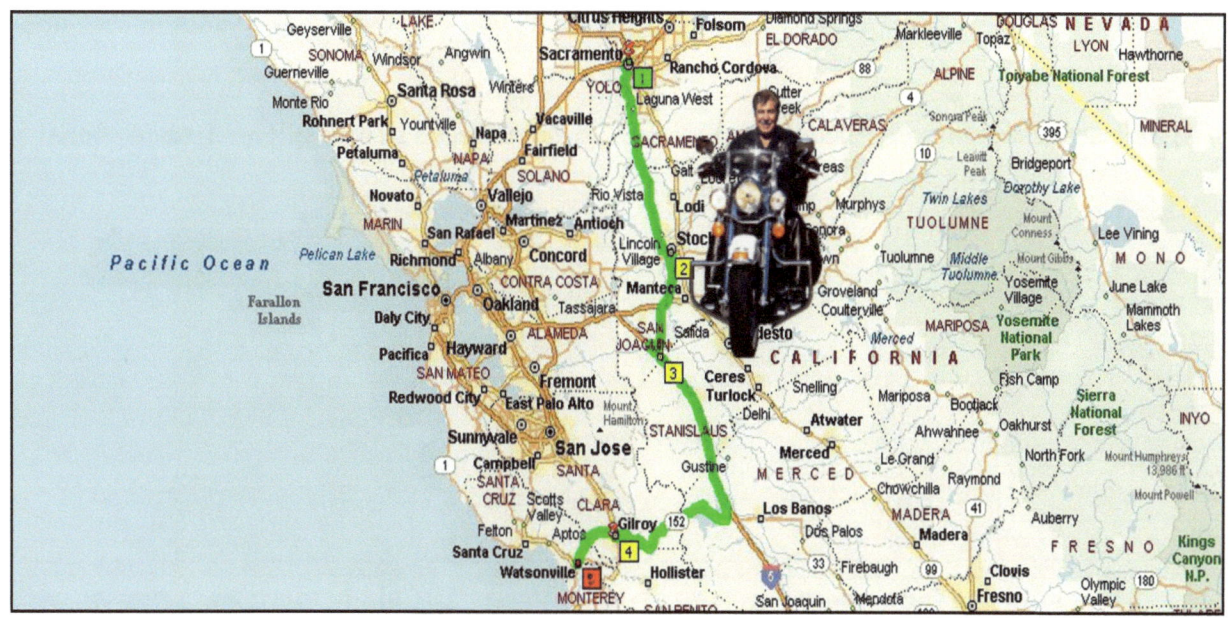

Sacramento, California to Watsonville, California

Day Fifteen … The Ride Home

I got up this morning and I decided to go see the old homestead and revisit old memories. But before doing that I decided to look through some magazines and information on Sacramento: *It was founded by Samuel Brannan and John Augustus Sutter, Jr., in 1848 around an embarcadero that Sutter Jr. constructed at the confluence of the American and Sacramento Rivers a few years prior. After the arrival of Europeans, the Nisenan branch of the Native American Maidu inhabited the Sacramento Valley area. The Spanish were the first to explore the area, and Sacramento fell into the Alta California province of New Spain when the conquistadors claimed Central America and the American Southwest for the Spanish Empire. The area was deemed unfit for colonization by a number of explorers, and as a result remained relatively untouched by the Europeans who claimed the region. When John Sutter arrived in the provincial colonial capital of Monterey in 1839, governor Juan Bautista Alvarado provided Sutter with the land he asked for and Sutter established New Helvetia, Which he controlled absolutely with a private army and relative autonomy from the newly independent Mexican government.*

The California Gold Rush started when gold was discovered at Sutter's Mill, one of Sutter, Sr.'s assets in the city of Coloma in 1848; the arrival of prospectors in droves ruined Sutter's New Helvetia, and trade began to develop around a wharf he had established where the American and Sacramento Rivers joined. In the region where Sutter had planned to establish the city of Sutterville, Sacramento City was founded; Sutter, Sr. put his son in charge in frustration, and Sutter, Jr. worked to organize the city in its growth. However, its location caused the city to periodically fill with water. Fires would also sweep through the city. To resolve the problems, the city worked to raise the sidewalks and buildings and began to replace wooden structures with more resilient materials, like brick and stone. The city was selected as the state capital in 1854 after Mariano Guadalupe Vallejo failed to convince the state government to remain in the city of his namesake.

After loading the Porker I headed out to the old homestead. It was still as I remembered it. Those were good times. (See Photos)

Must hold dog for a photo   **The old homestead**

Later, on my way out of town, I stopped by my old job where I used to work, Campbell Soup. (See Photos)

Campbell Soup   **Turning point**

Working there was one of the turning points in my life. But that story is for another time. I mounted up and gave Silver the spurs and we bolted on to the horrible freeways again and now we are heading home. I decided to stop in Gilroy and grab a margarita and some lunch. (See Photos)

WISHING YOU THE VERY BEST!!

I didn't want to get home and deal with making lunch for myself. I rode to the gas station and fed the Pork his chow, then I realized that while in California, after giving him his chow a number of times along the way, he never even burped once.

"Hey Pork, what's the story? You haven't sputtered, snorted or choked ever since we've been in California." "Oh that," he says, "I don't like foreign slop." "FOREIGN!!" I screamed. "You stupid pig we were in the USA, THE WHOLE TIME!!" "Well I only like California slop. I don't like their slop. It gives me indigestion." "INDIGESTION!! That's all it was and I spent all that money getting you fixed up." "Well I didn't ask you to." "Oh, by the way, when we get home I want you to clean up that pig pen of yours." "WHAT? I like my pig pen just the way it is. It's all muddy, slimy and dirty. "Oh yeah, well you're not going to attract any sow that way." "Oh yeah," he says, "they like me to be dirty." Oink, Oink, Oink, he's laughing and winking. "Stop it. I don't want to hear it," I said.

When we arrived at the old homestead, I put Silver in his stall and his mare is REAL HAPPY TO SEE HIM! Anyhow, I put Pork in his pig pen and he is totally in Hog Heaven rolling all around in his muddy mess. As I was walking to my front door I noticed a UPS package, I opened it and found this lovely painting of Pork by Alice Rivera, a dear friend of mine. How very thoughtful, I have wonderful friends. (See Painting)

I walked into the house and everything is as I left it more than two weeks ago. LIFE IS GOOD! All in all, a very good, short ride. I thought for a moment and remarked that the road gods were good to me, as I did not break down or get one ticket during my whole trip.

Well, I'm home now, at least for a spell and who knows? One day you might hear faintly outside your window, the sound of HI-O-SILVER . . . AWAAAAYYY. You will know that Joe and his stallion, Silver, and his sidekick, PorkChop are on another adventure to who knows where. Whichever way the wind is a-blowing, I reckon.

All I can say is: *Get your motor running get, out on the highway. Looking for adventure and whatever comes your way, Born to be wild, born to be wild. . . . Life is short, do it!

*My friends, I'll say it clear, I'll state my case, of which I am certain. "I've lived a life that's full, I've traveled each and every highway. And more, much more than this, I did it my way."

I did what I had to do, and saw it through without exemption, I planned each charted course, each careful step along the byway and more, much more than this, I did it my way.

But through it all when there was doubt, I ate it up and spit it out. I faced it all and I stood tall. And, I did it my way.

To think I did all that and may I say not in a shy way, oh no, oh no not me, I did it my way. The record shows I took the blows and did it my way.

Pork turn around! . . . "NO, it's the end!" . . . "BAD PIG!"

Yours Truly,
Joe Matus,
AKA, Lone Rider.

End Note

10/15/10 http://www.elkonevada.com/ Events & Attractions/Elko Area History p. 2

10/23/10 http://www.blm.gov/ut/st/en/fo/salt_lake/recreation/bonneville_salt_flats.html FAQ p.3

10/24/10 http://www.utah.com/cities/slc_history.htm p. 6

10/27/10 http://www.trainweb.org/wyomingrails/wylocales/wycasper.html p. 15

11/12/10 http://www.oglalalakotanation.org/OLN/Photos_BIA_Route_27_Dedication.html p. 23

11/23/10 http://www.blackhillsbadlands.com/home/citiestowns/badlandsregion/martin p. 27

11/28/10 http://en.wikipedia.org/wiki/On_the_Road_Again_(Willie_Nelson_song) p. 28

12/10/10 http://en.wikipedia.org/wiki/Rapid_City,_South_Dakota p. 32

12/26/10 http://www.sturgis-sd.org/ p. 33

01/18/11 http://archive.cyark.org/deadwood-info p. 42

01/20/11 http://www.thedoublehelixranch.com/ p. 49

01/22/11 http://en.wikipedia.org/wiki/Born_to_Be_Wild p. 53, 83, 96

08/16/03 Me and Pork, song written by Joe Matus and sung by Joe Matus p. 54

02/23/11 http://www.yellowstonenationalpark.com/history.htm p. 57

02/26/11 http://www.boisewiki.org/History_of_the_Boise_Region p. 70

02/27/11 http://www.lakevieworegon.org/ p. 79

05/12/11 http://en.wikipedia.org/wiki/Ashland,_Oregon#History p. 87

09/25/11 http://en.wikipedia.org/wiki/History_of_Sacramento,_California p. 93

11/06/11 http://en.wikipedia.org/wiki/My_Way_(song) p. 96

11/08/11 Microsoft Streets and Trips 2002

11/09/11 http://www.badpig.com

Author
Joe Matus

My two passions in life are flying my airplane and riding my Harley

∽

As a child I grew up in a little beach town called Santa Cruz, nestled between San Francisco and Monterey, California. I lost my parents early in life. Consequently, as a young child I had a different orientation to life than most young children. I spent a good deal of time alone and found my own way.

As a young boy I was intrigued with the idea of flight, so I built little model airplanes and hung them over my bed to play with. At night I would always twirl them around and around. Later, I was involved in flying radio controlled model airplanes. Finally, I was jumping off cliffs, hang gliding and I also flew sail planes. 40 years ago I joyously obtained my private pilot license.

Because I love adventure, I have tried rock climbing, spelunking, fencing, surfing, scuba, kayaking, and many other adventurous sports. Years ago I could not find an ocean kayak for surfing so I designed and built my own. I also had a keen interest in rivers so I designed and built a canoe. I have been on almost every river in California in both the kayak and canoe. Dirt biking finally introduced me to street bikes and I now own a Heritage Classic Harley Davidson Softail. If you have read the book I am sure you have already met "PorkChop."

I am currently semi-retired, having worked in the Insurance Industry for almost 40 years and I am also a Real Estate Agent.

www.ingramcontent.com/pod-product-compliance
Lightning Source LLC
Chambersburg PA
CBHW040822050726
47507CB00021B/106